AN
ORCA
YOUNG
READER

Long Shot

ERIC WALTERS

ORCA BOOK PUBLISHERS

National Library of Canada Cataloguing in Publication Data
Walters, Eric, 1957–
Long shot

"An Orca young reader"
ISBN 1-55143-216-1

I. Title.
PS8595.A598L66 2001   jC813'.54   C2001-910948-2
PZ7.W17129Lo 2001

Library of Congress Catalog Card Number: 2001092681

Orca Book Publishers gratefully acknowledges the support of
our publishing programs provided by the following agencies:
the Department of Canadian Heritage, The Canada Council
for the Arts, and the British Columbia Arts Council.

Cover design by Christine Toller
Cover and interior illustrations by John Mantha

IN CANADA
Orca Book Publishers
PO Box 5626, Station B
Victoria, BC Canada
V8R 6S4

IN THE UNITED STATES
Orca Book Publishers
PO Box 468
Custer, WA   USA
98240-0468

03 02 01 • 5 4 3 2 1

*For Mike Smith, Zack Alilovic,
Silvio Andrighetti, Fred Demers, and
Everton Allan — five gentlemen who know
you have to be a good person
to be a good coach.*

Chapter One

"I wish you'd quit squirming around in your seat, Nick," Kia said. "You're making me car sick."

"Then maybe you should stick your head out the window and get some fresh air," I answered. "Besides, I'm not squirming ... I'm just trying to get comfortable."

"You *are* squirming and you're making me uncomfortable. I don't know why you're so nervous."

"I'm not nervous ... well, not too nervous," I admitted.

"Don't try to change him," my mother piped in from the front seat. "Basketball makes him that way."

"It isn't basketball!" I snapped. "It's basketball try-outs. I hate try-outs!"

"It's no big deal," Kia said. "We go to the gym a few times and make the team. So what's the problem?"

"The problem is, what if we don't make the team?"

"We'll make it," she said reassuringly. "You have to be positive."

"I'm trying to be positive. It's just hard. Have you ever thought about how big this city is?"

"It's big … so what?"

"There are over half a million people who live here."

"I think it's closer to six hundred thousand … so?

"So let's just assume that most of those people are under a hundred years old."

"That's a pretty safe assumption," Kia agreed.

"And if you divide the whole population into one hundred age groups from babies to really old people. That would mean that you have half a million people … or six hundred thousand people divided into one hundred groups. Do you know what that means?"

"That you're spending *way* too much time thinking about long division?" Kia asked.

My mother chuckled.

"No, that there are at least six *thousand* kids in this city who are the same age as us."

"Much more than that," my mother piped in.

"No," I said, shaking my head. "Six hundred thousand divided by one hundred is six thousand."

"I'm not disagreeing with your math, but think

2

about it. There are a lot more people in certain age groups."

"There are?" I asked.

"Look around. Aren't there a lot more nine-year-olds around than ninety-nine-year-olds?" she asked.

"Your mother's right," Kia agreed. "So that must mean there are even *more* than six thousand kids in this city who are the same age as us."

"Great ... that makes me feel even better."

"I still don't get it," Kia said. "There are lots of kids our age. Big deal."

"It is a big deal!" I protested. "Are you telling me that, out of more than six thousand kids in this city, there aren't twelve kids who are better than us?"

"There weren't when we made the team last year," Kia said.

"Or the year before that when you were both on the travel team," my mother added.

"So that must mean we were among the twelve best players our age in the whole city for two years running," Kia said. "And nothing's changed."

"I guess you're right."

"Of course I'm right ... aren't I always?" Kia asked.

"I don't know about that, but I know you always *think* you're right."

"That's almost as good," she said. "And a lot better than not believing you're right when you are."

I had to admit she had me there. Kia was one

overflowing container of pure positivity. She completely believed in herself, always thinking she was right and that everything would always turn out for the best ... even when it didn't. Sometimes I thought that was one of her best qualities. Other times it just drove me crazy.

"Here we are," Mom said as she turned into the parking lot of the college where the try-outs were scheduled.

The parking lot was overflowing with cars. Half the cars would be for kids trying out for the younger team. Their try-out would be ending just as ours started. The other half of the crush of vehicles had brought kids who were trying to make the same team as us.

As we cruised the parking lot looking for a space, I saw a few familiar vehicles. On the back of several I spotted a 'Mississauga Magic' sticker attached to the bumper, just like our van. Those vehicles belonged to kids who had been on one of the rep teams last year — kids who would be on our team again this year I hoped.

"There's Coach's motor home!" Kia called out.

Coach Riley had a big, brown motor home that was almost as long as a bus. His rear bumper didn't just have a Magic bumper sticker on it. It was covered with stickers from places all across North America. He and his wife spent all summer travelling everywhere their motor home could travel. He used to joke that if it could float he'd have seen Europe by now.

"Where do you think Coach went this summer?" Kia asked.

"Could be anywhere, but I'm sure he'll tell us all about it."

"Do you think he brought us back some souvenirs like last year?" Kia asked.

"Probably," I said.

"He is such a nice man," Mom said as we wheeled into an empty space.

"The nicest," I agreed.

"And a good coach," she added.

"The best," Kia said. "But I guess coaching is like everything else … the more you do it the better you get."

"He certainly has had a lot of experience," my mother said.

Coach was retired now, but before that he was a high school gym teacher who coached all the teams at his school. His wife was still a teacher at that school.

"And besides everything else, he likes you two," Mom said.

"What's not to like?" Kia questioned as we climbed out of the car. "At least what's not to like about me?"

I shook my head. "Coach likes everybody on the team."

"I'm sure he does and that should make you both feel better," Mom said.

"How do you figure that?" I asked.

"Having the coach not only know you, but like you before you even walk into the gym can't be bad," she said.

She had a point there.

I slung my bag over my shoulder and we started to walk toward the gym. I glanced at my watch. It was ten minutes to one. That left me just enough time to take off my tear-aways, put on my basketball shoes, and do a little stretching before the practice started.

"This is as far as I go," Mom said. "Your Dad will be back to pick you two up at three ... okay?"

"Yeah ... sure ... thanks," I offered.

Mom knew that I didn't like anybody hanging around during these things. When Mom and Dad were sitting there it felt as if I had to have one eye on the ball and the other on them. Them being somewhere else, doing something else was better on everybody. Sometimes they even waited just outside the gym — as long as they were out of sight they were out of mind.

"Good luck."

"Thanks, I'll see at home later on," I said.

I watched as she turned and disappeared out the door of the building. Kia and I started in the opposite direction, weaving our way through the crowd of people. There were lots of parents — either waiting for the younger kids trying out in the gym right now — or standing with their kids who were going to go in with us. I recognized a lot of the kids. Some went to our school, or lived in the neighborhood, or played for other schools' teams, and a few I even knew from other try-outs, try-outs where they didn't make the team.

"Hey, look, there are the guys!" Kia said.

Up ahead were four of our teammates from last year. Even if I hadn't noticed their faces, I couldn't help but see what they were wearing. Jamie, D.J., Jordan, and Mark all had on their orange and white Magic shorts — the ones that our rep team wore last year. Of course Kia and I were also wearing ours. They were probably the ugliest looking shorts in the entire world ... and I was so proud of them.

The four guys were standing by the far doors leading into the gym. They had one of the doors partially opened and they were peeking in.

"I'm going to go and say hello," Kia said.

"Sure ... I'll see you inside."

Kia walked away. She knew that I wanted to be by myself anyway. She joined up with the guys and I watched as they started to laugh and joke around.

I never understood how people could be so relaxed when there was something as serious as basketball about to begin. It was time for me to get on both my shoes and my 'game face.'

I walked over to the side and slumped down against a wall, taking a seat on the floor. Slowly I opened up my bag and pulled out my basketball shoes — my new basketball shoes.

It was almost like a tradition in my family. Every fall I got a brand new pair of basketball shoes. They were just for practices and games. After the last game of the season they became my everyday shoes until they were worn down to nothing.

I pulled off my old shoes — last year's new shoes. I pulled my socks up, nice and tight. I didn't want any folds or creases. I slipped on one of the new ones, tightening the laces. I repeated the process with the second foot.

"Hello, Nick."

"Coach!" I exclaimed.

I got up to my feet and we shook hands.

"How have you been keeping yourself?" he asked.

"I'm fine … and you?"

"Never better. You looking forward to another season?" he asked.

"Yeah … sure … if I make the team," I said, fishing for some confirmation that I didn't have anything to worry about.

"Competition's going to be tough."

Those weren't exactly the words of encouragement I'd been looking for.

"Are *you* looking forward to another season?" I asked.

"Maybe more than any season I've ever had before," he said with a big smile.

"You are?"

"Most definitely."

He looked at his watch. "It's about time. Let's get inside where I can talk to everybody at once."

I followed after Coach Riley. He nodded to people as they offered their hands, or slapped him on the back, and said hello. Everybody knew and liked Coach.

We entered the gym just as the previous group of boys were gathering up their bags and water bottles and starting out to join their parents in the lobby.

At the far end I saw a dozen kids sitting on the gym floor at the feet of the coach in charge of that age group. I was positive I knew exactly what was going on. Those were kids who were being told that they weren't welcome to come back to the next try-out — they'd already been cut.

I wanted to look away, but I couldn't. It was like watching a car accident at the side of the road. I really shouldn't look over but something made it impossible not to look.

The coach said a few more words to them that I couldn't hear. Then they all got up and I could tell by the expressions on their faces that

I was probably right. Some of them looked angry, a couple confused, and one looked like he was going to start to cry. As they got close, I looked away. They deserved at least that much.

Probably the only thing worse than watching people have to go through that would have been going through it myself. So far every year I'd tried out I'd made the team ... would this year be different and, if it was, how would I react? I'd hate to cry in front of people.

A shrill whistle echoed through the gym and I looked over to where Coach Riley stood, in the middle of the floor. Kids started to slowly filter toward the center of the gym. I sprinted over full speed.

"Come on, bring it in!" yelled Coach and people started to move quickly.

I was already right by his side. So was Kia, and the rest of the guys from last year's team. I wasn't the only person who knew how much Coach hated people dawdling — 'wasting my valuable time' — he called it.

"And hold the balls!" he bellowed.

My ball was already tucked under my arm. I also knew how he felt about people bouncing a ball after he blew the whistle.

Maybe things like that were little but they were important things to know. Maybe they gave those of us who knew the Coach a little bit of an advantage.

"Good afternoon, it's good to see so many familiar faces," Coach started to say. "As well as so many new ones."

I looked around. I recognized a lot of people — all my old teammates — but there were a whole lot I didn't know ... kids who looked older, or at least bigger, than I was.

"I want to start off with a couple of announcements before we go any further."

He probably wanted to tell us about the way the try-outs would be run, and, how no matter whether we made it or not, we were still —

"You all know that I have a great love for the game of basketball," Coach said.

Nobody could argue with that.

"And I believe we have the potential to have a fantastic team for this coming year." He paused. "Maybe even better than the wonderful team I had the honor of coaching last year."

He paused and looked right at where Kia and I and a few of the other guys stood and he gave us a smile. That made me feel better about how things were going to go. We were a good team — a very good team — and we were good players. I was a good player.

"So it's with regret that I am announcing that I will not be your coach for the coming year."

Chapter Two

"What?" I gasped. "What did you say?"

"I'm not going to coach the team."

"Quit joking around, Coach," Kia said.

"I'm not joking, Kia. I won't be your coach this year."

"Why not ... why won't you be the coach?" I asked, my voice hardly a whisper.

"Because it will be hard to coach when I'm hundreds or even thousands of miles away from here."

"How ... why?" somebody asked.

"The how will be in my motor home. The why is because my wife has retired, and she and I are now free to pursue our love of travelling." He paused and looked at his watch. "Starting in about fifteen minutes."

"You're leaving today?" Kia asked.

"My wife is waiting in our vehicle. We'll be a

hundred miles south of here before your first try-out is even finished."

"But we have to have a coach," I said.

"Who will coach the team?" Kia asked.

"That's all been taken care of, Kia. I'd like to introduce you ... all of you, to the new coach."

A man who was about the age of my father had been standing off to one side. He now stepped up beside Coach. He wore track pants, a T-shirt, and had a whistle around his neck. He certainly looked like a coach. He also looked familiar. I didn't know where, but I thought I'd seen him before ... but where?

"Players and parents, I'd like to introduce Mr. Len Barkley."

That name sounded familiar as well.

The man — Mr. Barkley — gave a little wave.

"I've know Len a long time. We first met twenty-one years ago when he was in grade nine and tried out for the senior basketball team. I told him that he was more than welcome to try out for the team but that he would be better served to go to the junior team try-outs." Coach paused. "He didn't listen. He not only tried out, but made that team and became a starter. Len was a starter for four straight years and in his senior year we were fortunate to have him lead us to the championship."

"I was the fortunate one," Mr. Barkley said.

"Fortunate to have had Coach Riley be there to teach me about basketball."

"And," Coach continued, "Len went on to play university ball on a full scholarship for four years and led his team to three league titles."

"I was injured and missed the last half of my senior year or it would have been *four* titles in *four* seasons," Mr. Barkley said.

Coach laughed. "Len has never been accused of lacking confidence." He paused. "He was a great player and one of the most knowledgeable basketball minds around. This man knows the game."

"I've learned from the best," the new coach said.

"He's only recently moved back to our city. He spent most of his adult life elsewhere, having established a very successful business in the city where he played for parts of two seasons with the —"

"That's more than enough about me," Mr. Barkley said, cutting him off. "Instead I'd like us all to take a minute to say thank you to a special man for all that he's done for the kids and students of this community. Can we all give Coach Riley the big round of applause that he so richly deserves?"

Mr. Barkley started to clap his hands and everybody in the gym joined in and began to clap and cheer. Coach shyly smiled and looked down at his feet as the clapping got louder and louder and louder. Finally he raised his hands and tried to quiet the crowd.

"Thank you! Thank you all!" he called out and we stopped clapping. "I'm going to miss you all ... very much ... very much," he said, choking over the last few words.

"I think he's going to cry," Kia whispered.

I was going to say something, but I wasn't completely sure that I wasn't going to cry too.

"I've taken enough of your time here today. I've got places to go and you've got basketball to play."

All of a sudden people began to clap and cheer again. Coach came over and started to shake the hands of each of the players from last year. He reached Kia and gave her a hug as well as shaking her hand. I was next.

"I wish you all the best, Nick," he said.

"And you too, Coach ... and thanks for everything."

He smiled. "It was a pleasure to coach such a fine young man. You take care of yourself. And Nick ... play hard."

He shook hands with the rest of the players and then started to slip off to the side. Slowly he moved through the crowd, shaking hands and saying goodbye. I watched until he reached the door and then disappeared.

I couldn't help but think how much I was going to miss having him around and —

A loud shrill whistle blast brought me back

to the present. All eyes in the gym focused on Mr. Barkley.

"This is a closed try-out!" he yelled. "All those who aren't trying out for the team are to leave the gym! And that includes all — I repeat *all* — parents! Your kids will meet you outside the doors at three o'clock!"

Wow I liked that! I hated parents, my own or anybody else's, gawking and staring and comparing me and every other kid in the gym to their kid. It felt like you were a science experiment and everything you did was under some sort of microscope.

Slowly people started to move toward the door of the gym.

"And everybody who's not leaving should start running!" he yelled. "Five laps ... half speed ... then five laps full speed. Let's do it!"

I fell into line along with Kia and everybody else and we started to jog around the outside of the gym.

"Didn't see that one coming," Kia puffed.

"Nope. Hope it's going to be okay."

"Why wouldn't it be —"

"Less talking and more running!" he called out.

I fell into line behind Kia and concentrated on running.

I watched the last of the parents file out of the gym and then saw Mr. Barkley pull the door closed.

Not only weren't they going to be in the gym, they weren't even going to be peeking into it.

"Pick it up!" he yelled. "I said first five were at half-speed, not snail speed!"

The line started to move more quickly. Kia and I were somewhere in the middle of the pack — a very large pack. With nothing else to do I focused on the other kids in the gym. There were a lot of them. More than I ever remembered before. There were also a lot of people I didn't recognize. Who were these kids and where did they come from?

The line started to move more quickly as the first in line finished the fifth lap. Like a long snake the speed change passed down the line until it reached me. I dug in deeper. Within a lap Kia and I were passing people — kids who didn't have the legs or lungs to keep up the pace. That felt good. I always liked to end up close to the front. I kept my eyes trained on Kia right ahead and trailed behind her and — somebody whisked by me on the outside and then passed Kia! That wasn't supposed to be happening. He was no more than a few feet ahead of her when Kia did exactly what I knew she'd do — she kicked it into a higher gear and started after him. I kept my eyes on Kia and ran with her.

This kid — I'd never seen him before — wove his way past another kid and then another, and another. We passed the runner at the head of the line, really digging deep, but even though we were passing other kids the gap between us and the other kid was still growing. Whoever he was, he was fast. We weren't going to be catching him in the half lap we had left. At least nobody else was going to be — another player shot by us, even though we were running nearly at a sprint. I wanted to catch him, but I had nothing left. I slowed down as we reached the finish and then dropped down to a walk.

Behind me other kids finished up. Some of them came to a complete stop or were doubling over. A couple walked over to the bench and grabbed their water bottles and —

"I didn't call for a water break!" Mr. Barkley yelled and the two guys put their bottles back down.

"Hurry it up!" he bellowed. "This ain't no walk in the park! If this run is too much for you, maybe you should just gather up your stuff and leave now!"

Looking at all the bodies filling the gym I would have been happy if about half of them *would* just leave. Of course, anybody who left now wouldn't have been anybody to worry about anyway.

"Gather around," Mr. Barkley called out as the last few stragglers finished their laps.

I got there fast and stood directly in front of him.

"When I call you in, I want you to run — just like that kid did," he said, pointing at me.

Everybody was staring at me. I felt embarrassed and pleased at the same time.

"Anybody who doesn't come will cost everybody laps. I want to start by setting up some ground rules," he said. "I am the coach of this team and none of you or your parents are my assistant coaches. I don't want any opinions or ideas or disagreements. What I say is law and I am the judge and jury. If you don't like it, then too bad!"

Kia looked at me and I knew exactly what she was thinking — that was so different than Coach Riley.

"You will address me as Coach, or Mr. Barkley, or simply as sir. Nothing else is acceptable. I am not your pal, or next door neighbor or your mommy. Do you all understand?"

I didn't think there was any danger of mistaking him for my mother — or a pal.

"When I blow my whistle, you stop whatever it is that you're doing. I don't want to hear anything, including the sound of bouncing balls. Your eyes, ears, and attention will be on me."

There was a collective nodding of heads.

"Most of you know, and many of you have played for Coach Riley. I want you to know that I have a great deal of respect for him."

My ears perked up — whenever somebody

said something like that I was always waiting for a "but."

"But there are many things that I'm going to be doing differently."

Part of me was proud I could predict what he was going to say — the other part was worried what he meant by 'different.'

"I don't believe you can practice soft and then play hard, so my practices are going to be harder, more demanding, and more physical than most of you have ever experienced. When you're through with one of my practices, you're going to know you've been worked. You may even think you've been through a war. I'm doing that for your own good, although, when you're holding your gut or feeling the burn, you may not think so. Being nice as either a player or a coach doesn't win basketball games and we're here to win games. Now, enough talking. Time to move. I want six lines, about ten players per line. We're going to start with suicides! Raise your hand if you know what a suicide drill involves!"

About half of us raised our hands.

"For those who don't know, you run full speed to the foul line, touch the floor, and come back to the base line. Then full speed to half court, touch the floor, and race back to the base. Then to the far foul line and back, and finally all the way coast to coast at full speed."

A groan went up from some of the players.

"I told you I wasn't looking for any assistant coaches. That groan will cost you all five more laps!"

A couple of people in the back grumbled.

"Make that seven more laps!" he bellowed. "Anybody want to make it ten?"

There was dead silence.

"Good. Now get running!"

★ ★ ★

"Everybody gather around!" Coach Barkley yelled.

I grabbed my ball and moved as quickly as I could to his side. I wasn't moving nearly as quickly as I had two hours before, but quicker than most of the other kids. A few hadn't been able to handle the pace and had to sit out. Others weren't given a chance to find out.

Before the try-out was even half way through Coach Barkley started to make cuts — at least I was pretty sure they were cuts.

At first I didn't even know what was happening. I saw him call this kid over to talk to him. I thought he was just asking him something or giving him some advice or suggesting how he could do something better. Then I saw the kid go off to the far end of the gym. Then I saw him go up to a second kid, and a third and a fourth, and send them down there too. They were shooting hoops at one of the nets. He wandered down there a few times but basically he left them alone. I could tell myself that none of those guys were very good, but they should have at least had the chance to last the whole first try-out. It got to the point that when the coach even looked my way I got nervous.

We all stood around Coach Barkley.

"Lots of you have been making very basic, very fundamental errors. I've spoken to many of you about those mistakes," he said.

I looked away. I didn't know about all the others but he'd spoken to me about my jump shot. He said my legs weren't straight enough and that was why I was aiming off to the side. After he'd spoken to me, I'd tried to do it his way, but it seemed to throw off my whole shot. I was aiming straighter but coming up too short or too long.

"I want to make it clear that a mistake is only a mistake if you don't learn from it. If I've made a suggestion, then you should spend time — and I mean a lot of time — working on it between now and the next try-out. I hate, I repeat *hate*, telling people the same thing more then once."

He didn't have to tell me that twice. I'd be out on the driveway working on it until I could do what he wanted. I figured it might even be better to miss a shot using the technique he'd shown me rather than making one my way.

"That's it for today. Your parents are waiting for you outside," Coach Barkley said. "Some of you will be hearing from me between now and the next week. If you don't get a phone call, you're welcome to come back to the second try-out."

Great! Now I got to spend the entire week cringing every time the telephone rang. I started to walk away.

"Could last year's team please remain behind for a few minutes?" he called out.

I stopped and spun around. What did he want to say to us? I looked at Kia and she gave me a 'don't worry' look. That was easy for her. She never worried about anything.

We all filtered back as the rest of the kids moved off to the side, gathered their things, and started out of the gym.

"I want to tell you players that my expectations are going to be higher for you," Coach Barkley said. "Since you've all played a lot of ball, I think you should know the basics and, if you don't, then something is wrong."

I thought about my jump shot. Was he talking about me?

"I'm going to be slightly more tolerant of new players. If they don't know something, it might be because nobody ever told them before. For you players, I suspect if you don't know, then you refused to listen to your coach or you simply can't do it."

I stared so hard at the spot on the floor in front of me I wondered if I was going to burn a hole through the hardwood.

"I also see that you all wore your Magic shorts from last year," he said. "This will be the last time that happens during these try-outs."

"What do you mean?" one of the guys asked.

"What I mean is that I don't want you — any of you — wearing those shorts or your jerseys to my try-outs again. It isn't just the try-outs that are going to change, but the roster too. It's a long shot that you're all going to be here at the end of these try-outs. Last year's team is gone. You get on my team because of what you do this year and not because of what happened last year. Now gather up your stuff, the next squad needs the gym."

We started off once again.

"He's a fun guy," Kia said.

"You have a strange idea of fun," I said quietly.

I looked back over my shoulder. Coach Barkley was gathering up balls and stuffing them into a net bag. He had a noticeable limp when he walked. I'd thought he was limping slightly at the beginning of the practice, but it definitely got worse during the two hours.

"So just how worried are you?" Kia asked.

"Didn't you hear what he said?" I asked in return.

"Of course, I did, but we don't have to worry. We're both good players."

"We're all good players," D.J. said as he peered over Kia's shoulder.

"Yeah, third best team in the whole region last year," Jamie piped in.

Something told me that Mr. Barkley was not the sort of guy who'd be happy with third place. Or second. Actually I didn't think he'd even be what you'd call happy if we finished first. He just didn't seem like a really happy guy.

"Anyway, he's probably just talking," Kia said. "Saying things to make us work harder. I don't think anybody has anything to worry about."

"I hope you're right," I said, although I was pretty sure she wasn't. This guy didn't seem like somebody who said one thing and did another.

"Look over there," Kia said.

I turned around. Coach Barkley was talking to some kid who'd been slow getting his stuff and getting out of the gym. We couldn't hear what he was saying, but judging from the way he was gesturing and the expression on his face, he wasn't too happy.

"Let's get out of here fast before he wants to say anything more to us," I said.

Chapter Three

"How did things go?" my father asked as we jumped into the back seat of the car.

"Terrible ... awful," I muttered as I pulled the door closed.

"Come on, Nick, they couldn't have been *that* bad," he said as we started to drive away.

"Yes, it was," Kia said. "It was bad."

"I can't imagine Coach Riley running a bad try-out."

"He didn't run anything except the engine of his motor home," I said.

"His motor home? What do you mean?" my father asked.

"Coach isn't our coach anymore. He's quit," Kia explained.

"He's retired to travel," I added.

"Wow, I can't believe that ... his whole life is basketball."

"And travelling. And that's what he's doing right now, him and his wife," Kia said.

"He said goodbye to us and then got in his motor home and drove off."

"He seemed pretty happy about it," Kia said.

"Except he was crying at the end," I said, not mentioning how close I had been to tears too.

"I guess we should be happy for him," my father said.

"I guess so," I agreed, although that sounded more like something my mother would say instead of my father.

"So who's in charge of the team?" my father asked.

Now that sounded more like him.

"Some guy."

"He must have a name."

"Three of them. Sir, Coach, and Mr. Barkley," Kia said.

"Did he run a good try-out?"

"A tiring one. He had us running laps and doing suicides and —"

"And any time anybody even coughed he gave us all more laps to run."

"Sounds like he's tough."

"Tough doesn't even begin to describe him," I said. "He's already made the first cuts ... during the try-outs."

"He did?" my father asked.

"I think so ... although some of them probably didn't even know they were cut."

"I don't understand, how can they not know they were cut?" my father asked.

"He picked out some players and sent them down to the far end of the gym, away from where the rest of us were trying out," I explained.

"I saw that too," Kia said. "They were all the weaker players."

"It was too fast. He didn't even give them a chance," I said.

"But aren't you the one who complained that Coach Riley always waited too long and kept kids around who had no chance to make the team?"

"Well ..." I actually had always complained about that. I thought it was better for those kids to die in one quick blow rather than sort of linger around thinking they had a chance when everybody knew they didn't.

"And he said that he didn't want us to wear any part of our Magic uniform to the try-outs," Kia said. "That just because we were on the team last year doesn't mean we're going to be on the team this year."

"That's fair," my father agreed. "Every year is a new year and you have to make the team on merit."

"And he also said that our team last year was too soft and too nice," I said.

"Hmm ... that's interesting," my father said quietly.

"What do you mean by that?" I asked.

"Well ... you know how much I respected Coach Riley," he began.

"But what?" I asked, knowing something had to follow.

"But at times I thought that he could have been harder on you guys."

"What do you mean?"

"Things like making you run more in practices."

"We ran in practices," I argued.

"As hard as you did today?" he asked.

"Not really," I reluctantly admitted. "But what else?"

"He was so quiet on the sidelines. It would have helped to yell out more instructions or to tell somebody — loudly — if they were making a mistake."

"This guy has got no problem pointing out mistakes," Kia said with a smirk.

I didn't want to go there right now. "So you wanted him to yell at us more?"

"And I think you all could have been more aggressive. Sometimes I think your team was just too nice," my father said.

"That's what this new coach said too," Kia explained.

I looked up and saw the smirk on my father's face in the rear view mirror.

"There are always changes when a new coach takes over," my father said. "The important thing is, does he know about basketball?"

"I think he does," Kia said. "He made some good suggestions and the drills were good."

"And Coach Riley said he knew the game," I added.

"Was your old coach part of picking the new guy?" my father asked.

"I think so. He's known him for years. He said he coached him in high school," Kia said.

"And that he went on to play at university for four years and led his team to a bunch of championships."

"So it sounds like he knows basketball and ..." my father paused. "What did you say his name was?"

"Barkley."

"Len Barkley?" he asked.

"I think that was it," I said.

"I thought it was Ken," Kia added.

"No, I'm pretty sure it's Len," I disagreed.

"And how old is he?" my father asked as he pulled the car to a stop in our driveway.

"I don't know ... it's hard to tell with adults," I said.

My father turned around in his seat. "Is he

around my age?" he demanded excitedly.

"Sure ... maybe ... he could be," I said.

"If I'm right, do either of you two have any idea who your coach is?"

"No, who?" I demanded.

"Yeah, who is he?"

Without answering my father jumped out of the car and slammed the door shut. Kia and I looked at each other in shock.

"What's wrong with your father?" Kia demanded.

"I don't know! Come on!"

We leaped out of the car, and chased after him. He was already in the house before we got close. I pulled open the door and charged into the house.

"Dad! Where are you?" I yelled.

My mother poked her head out of the living room and gave me a disapproving look.

"Do you know where Dad is?"

"I hoped he was with you . . . he did drive you two home, didn't he?"

"He did, but then he said something about our new coach, and then —"

"You have a new coach?" she asked.

"Yeah, but then he ran into the house and —"

"Your new coach?"

"No, Dad. He ran into the house and —"

"I found it!" Dad yelled as he came running up the stairs from the basement. "Here it is!"

He was waving something in the air.

"Is this your coach?" he asked as he passed a magazine to me.

I looked down at the page. There in the middle of an article was a picture of Mr. Barkley.

"Yeah, that's him," I confirmed.

"Let me see," Kia said, pushing in to see the picture.

"My goodness!" my father practically yelled. "You're being coached by Len Barkley!"

"Who's Len Barkley?" my mother asked.

"He's the new coach of the team!" my father sang out.

"I gathered that, but who is he?" she asked.

"And why is he in some magazine?" Kia asked.

"He's not in *some* magazine. He's in this month's *Sports Illustrated* !"

"But why is he in *Sports Illustrated* ?" Kia asked.

"Because he's Len Barkley!" my father exclaimed.

"I think we all understand what his name is," my mother said. "But who is he and why is he in *Sports Illustrated*?"

"It's a special feature each issue called 'Catching Up With' and he's this month's celebrity," my father explained.

I'd glanced at the article when this issue arrived at the house. Maybe that's why his picture and name seemed familiar to me.

"But why does anybody want to catch up with him?" my mother asked.

"Because he's Len Barkley! He was on the cover of *Sports Illustrated* twenty years ago. Don't any of you know who he is?"

"*If* we knew, we wouldn't be asking you," she said.

"I'd looked at it a bit," I admitted. It was usually the last thing I read in each issue. It was always about people I'd never heard of. My father, on the other hand, loved that feature.

"Len Barkley is probably the best basketball player this city ever produced," my father explained.

"He is?" I asked.

"I even played against him one game. He was a senior on one of your old coach's teams and my school played against them."

"Did you win?" I asked.

"Win? Nobody won against them. Barkley was like a one man wrecking crew! He scored more than thirty points, had a dozen assists and that many rebounds, and I think he put two of our players out of the game with injuries."

"I can't believe that," my mother said.

"No, he was really that good."

"I don't mean that. I mean that you can't ever remember to pick up the three things I send you to the store to buy and you can remember his statistics from a game more than twenty years ago?" my mother asked in amazement.

"I'll never forget that game," my father said. "Would either of you ever forget if you played against Julius the Jewel Johnson?"

"Of course not," I agreed. "But we're not talking about the Jewel, just some high school player."

"Some high school player?" my father questioned, sounding offended. "He was probably the best high school player of all time! A player who went on to university where he lead his team to three, count them, three national titles! Something that nobody, including Julius Johnson, ever did ... something that nobody will probably ever do again."

"If he's that good, how come we've never heard of him?" Kia asked.

"Probably because it was long before either of you were born," my mother said.

"But I know lots of players who played before I was born," I said. "People like Wilt Chamberlain, and Kareem Abdul-Jabar, Dr. J., Magic Johnson, Bill Russell, and of course Jordan and —"

"But they all had long careers in the pro's," my father said. "Barkley didn't play ... except for a couple of games."

"I don't understand," I said. "If he was that good, then why didn't he make the pro's?"

"Because of an injury."

"The one he got in his senior year?" I asked.

"Yeah ... how did you know about that?" my father questioned.

"He mentioned that he had some sort of injury that stopped him from leading his team one year."

"His senior year. They were the odds-on favorite to win it all again when he got injured."

"Was it a bad injury?" my mother asked.

"I still remember seeing it on TV," my father said, shaking his head slowly. "It was probably the worst injury I've ever seen."

"What happened?"

"There was a loose ball and Barkley and a couple of other guys were all scrambling for it and somehow they all got twisted around and somebody came down on his ankle."

"Was it broken?" Kia asked.

"Not broken. It was shattered so badly that he was never able to play again."

"Ever?" I questioned in amazement.

"Never the same way. He was drafted and played a few games the next year in the pro's but he was never able to play the way he had before the injury. So after having surgery a couple of times and playing in a handful of games over that first season, he retired."

"That's too bad," Kia said.

"Do you know what I remember most about the whole thing?" my father asked.

"Playing against him in high school?" I asked.

He shook his head. "It was what happened after the injury. It was a nationally televised game. Barkley was lying there on the floor and the camera captured his face and it looked like he was in unbelievable pain."

"It would have been incredibly painful," my mother agreed.

"But through it all he never let go of the ball."

"What do you mean?" I asked.

"He got the ball in the scramble. He was taken out of the arena by stretcher ... and he still had the ball in his hands. He wouldn't let go of it ... wouldn't even give it to the referees. That's the sort of player he was."

My father paused. "You know ... he could have been the very best ... could have been."

Chapter Four

I sat at the desk in my room staring at the article. I should have been doing my homework, but instead I'd read it five or six times. Now I was just staring at the pictures – there were two.

One was of Coach Barkley, taken within the last few weeks or months. He looked pretty much like he did now — a tall middle-aged sort of guy. In the picture he was casually dressed, a sort of smirk on his face and his forehead extended way up his head where there used to be hair. He looked like somebody who lived in the neighborhood or worked at the grocery store or was somebody's father.

The other picture was different. It was the cover from the old *Sports Illustrated*. It had Coach Barkley out on a basketball court, looking like he was maybe twenty years old. There was another player as well. He was wearing a different uniform and they were fighting for a rebound. In big red letters on the picture it said, 'Barkley wins another one!'

I'd read the article over and over. It was funny how I almost always read each *Sports Illustrated* cover to cover, but hardly ever read that feature. It was always about some old guy I'd never heard of. Of course, it was different this time. I hadn't just read it, I'd almost memorized it.

It talked all about the things Coach Riley and my father had told Kia and me. About what a great player and a leader Coach Barkley was and how he always led his teams to victory. About how hard he worked and —

"You through with your homework?"

At the sound of my mother's voice I quickly pushed the magazine under my math book and turned to see her standing at the door.

"Almost."

She gave me a questioning look. She walked over and pulled the magazine out from its hiding spot.

"Have you even *started* your homework?"

"Just getting ready to start," I answered reluctantly.

"If you haven't even started, then how can it be almost done?"

"It's like you always said, the hardest part of anything is beginning it ... so, since I'm almost ready to start, I'm almost through the hardest part."

"Very funny. Haven't you finished that article yet?"

"I've read it a few times."

"Then what's so fascinating about it?" Mom asked.

"It's just strange having a coach who's a celebrity ... or would have been a celebrity."

"So what's he like?"

"I don't really know ... he didn't really talk to us much during the try-out."

"What does the *article* say," she said, pointing at the magazine.

"Oh ... lots of things."

"Such as?" she asked.

"It uses a lot of different words to describe him. Things like he was a fighter, and fearless and relentless."

"Sounds more like he was a soldier than a basketball player."

"He was also called a killer," I said.

"How pleasant," my mother said sarcastically. "And just how was he a killer?"

"It described how he would throw himself into the stands to get a loose ball, or stand there and take a charge, or stand toe to toe with guys who were a lot bigger than him. He really played to win."

"And some people play to lose?" my mother asked with a laugh.

"You know what I mean. He was very competitive."

"As opposed to you and your father?"

She always thought that the two of us were too competitive and took basketball much, much too seriously.

"Does it say anything about the injury that ended his career?" Mom asked.

"Yep. The guy who wrote the article was there that night. It was like Dad remembered."

"And does it say what he's been doing for the past twenty years since the injury?"

"Running some sort of business ... it says he's been a 'successful businessman'."

"Did he stay involved in basketball?" she asked.

I shook my head. "It said that he found it too hard to watch so he didn't have anything to do with the game for a long time. He didn't even watch it on TV or read about it in the newspapers for years and years. It said it's only the past few years, since his son started playing, that he's gotten interested again.

"How old is his son?"

"It doesn't say."

"Could he have been at the try-outs?"

"Could have been," I said. There were a couple of people who I didn't know and one of them could have been his son.

My mother looked at the article. Being a writer

she was always interested in how something was written, even if she wasn't interested in what was written. She always said that *Sports Illustrated* had some of the best writers in the world, and it was unfortunate that they were wasting their time writing about sports when there were so many more interesting and important things to write about.

More important I could maybe understand. More interesting than sports wasn't possible.

"Oh, that's sad," she said.

"What's sad?"

"This line … 'and he may very well be the best player who never was'," she said.

"How's that sad? Everybody said he was a great player."

"Who never had the chance to show that to everybody," she said.

"He did for a while … all through high school and university. That was Dad's dream to have played for his university."

"That's your Dad's dream, but that doesn't mean it was your new coach's dream."

"I don't understand."

"His whole life, probably since he was younger than you are now, basketball was the biggest thing in his life. Wouldn't you agree?" she asked.

"Yeah, sure."

"And every step of the way he probably was

incredibly successful. What do you think his dream was?"

"To make it to the NBA and ..." I stopped myself. It was so obvious.

"And he only got to live that dream for seven games. There he was at maybe twenty-one or twenty-two years of age and the thing he probably spent his life dreaming of was over." She paused. "Where do you go from there?"

I hadn't thought about it that way. It would have been hard to have all that taken away from you.

"I should let you get back to work ... or should I say *get* to work," Mom said.

"I guess I should get going."

Mom handed me back the article and started to walk away. She stopped at the doorway.

"Nicky, do you think you're going to make this team?" she asked.

"I hope so ... maybe ... I guess."

"And if you don't?" she asked.

"I don't even want to think about it," I admitted.

"But if you didn't make the team ... if you never made any team ever again ... would you still like basketball?"

"I'm sure I could make some team somewhere and —"

"I know you could, but if you couldn't?" she asked. "Would you still like basketball? Would you still fool around on the driveway? Would you still watch it on TV and want to go to the games with your Dad?"

I didn't know what to say or what she wanted me to say.

"That's okay," Mom said. "That probably isn't a fair question to ask you."

I let out a big sigh of relief.

"Do you think a nice big cup of hot chocolate might get you working again?" she asked.

"It couldn't hurt."

"Good, I'll fix us both a cup and then bring yours up to you."

"Thanks."

My mother started out the door.

"Mom!"

She turned around.

"I'd still play, even if it was by myself on the driveway. I just like basketball."

She beamed, rushed into the room and planted a big kiss on the side of my face.

"What was that for?" I asked, wiping my cheek with the back of my hand.

"That was for being wonderful. So wonderful that you deserve some miniature marshmallows with that hot chocolate of yours."

I wasn't sure what I'd done that was so wonderful, but I did know I wasn't going to argue about anything that involved me getting miniature marshmallows.

Chapter Five

We slowed down as we came up to Kia's house. We had no sooner pulled into the driveway when she came running out to meet us. She opened the back door.

"Hi," she sang out as she jumped in beside me and pulled the door closed.

"You sound like you're in a good mood," my father said.

"I'm looking forward to playing a little b-ball," she said. "How about you?"

"I'm just glad I'm going back."

Kia only shook her head.

I knew what she was thinking, of course. She knew I was worried about getting a call telling me I'd been cut. Kia was sure that neither of us was going to be called. I knew in my head that she was right, but my gut had other ideas.

For the entire week I'd dreaded a phone call

from Coach Barkley — a call to tell me that I wasn't invited to come back to the next try-out. Every time the phone rang that was the first thought that popped into my mind. It wasn't until I was out the door, in the car, and driving away toward the gym today that I was one hundred percent certain that I was okay.

"I was thinking about dropping in with you two today," my father said.

"You can leave us at the door," I suggested.

"I just want to make sure you get in okay."

"We always get in okay. You know I don't like you or Mom being there," I said.

"I just wanted to come in and watch for a few minutes."

"You can't," I said.

"I promise not to say anything to you, I just want to watch for a while," my father said. "You won't even know I'm there."

"No, you don't understand. You aren't *allowed* to watch."

"Not allowed?" my father questioned.

"Coach Barkley doesn't want any parents in the gym during the try-outs."

"None at all?" my father questioned.

"He made everybody leave right away," I said.

"He even closed the doors so nobody could peek in," Kia added.

"Oh … that's too bad … too bad."

"It's no big problem. You haven't been to a try-out or a practice for a long time." I paused. "Then again, you don't even want to be there to see me, do you?"

"Of course, I want to see you play!" he protested. "I just thought that since I was there anyway, I could say hello to your coach."

"Say hello to him?"

"Yeah, mention how much I used to enjoy watching him ... maybe tell him I played against him once."

"Sounds like you want to ask him for his autograph," I joked.

"I was thinking that if he didn't mind he might be willing to sign my *Sports Illustrated*," my father said, grabbing it off the seat and holding it up.

"You brought along your magazine?" I asked in amazement.

"Sure ... it would only take him a couple of seconds."

"Please don't do that, Dad! It would be so ... so ..."

"Embarrassing?" Kia asked.

"Yes, embarrassing. Please don't do it!"

My father didn't answer right away. "I don't think he'd really mind, but, if that's how you feel, I won't do it. At least for now."

"Thank you."

There was enough to be worried about without

having things complicated by my father asking for autographs.

My stomach tightened as the gym appeared up ahead. There wasn't any more time left for this conversation.

"Is it all right with you two if I bring the vehicle to a full stop or would you like me to just slow down and you can jump out?" my father asked.

"You can stop," I said, "but don't turn off the engine."

Kia giggled and I looked up at the rear view mirror and saw a smile crease my father's face. That was good. I hadn't wanted him to come in and embarrass me but I didn't want to hurt his feelings either.

Kia climbed out. "Thanks for the ride," she said.

"Yeah, thanks, Dad."

"No problem. Play hard and good luck."

"Thanks," I said as I went to close the door.

"Nick!" he called out and I held the door.

"You think you might be able to use these?" he asked, holding up my shoes.

"Thanks!" I called out as I grabbed them. "Thanks a lot!"

He smiled. "I'll be back in two hours. I'll be waiting in the car ... way over there," he said, pointing to the far end of the parking lot.

I couldn't help but smile back. "Thanks again."

I turned around and hurried after Kia who was

already inside the front door of the building.

There were a lot of people waiting outside the gym but it was obvious that there were a lot fewer than last week. I scanned the crowd looking for our friends. Had they made the cut? Quickly I was able to pick out three ... four ... six ... seven ... eight guys — everybody was all here!

I hadn't wanted to call anybody all week. What would I say to them if they told me they'd been cut? I knew I wouldn't know what to say to them if I'd been called and told not to come back. Thank goodness everybody had made it at least this far.

"Hi, guys!" I yelled as I rushed up to them.

"Hi, Nick ... What's happening? ... Good to see you," various people mumbled.

Kia gave me a confused look. She knew it wasn't like me to come up and start talking to people before a try-out. I was just so glad to see everybody was still here.

"Boy, he's cut a lot of people already," D.J. said.

"He's going for quality instead of quantity," Kia joked.

"There's no point in inviting back people who have no chance," Jamie said. "It's just wasting their time and getting their hopes up for no reason."

"I guess you're right," I agreed.

"I see everybody remembered not to wear their uniform this week," Kia said.

Everybody was dressed in a different combination of shirt and shorts — none of which even had a hint of Magic orange.

"I almost forgot what he'd said to us last week," D.J. admitted. "I was half way out to the car before I remembered and ran back to change."

"It would have been okay either way," I said.

"I don't think so," Kia said.

"Neither do I," Jamie agreed. "I betcha he would have cut D.J. on the spot if he'd worn his Magic stuff."

"Maybe, but that's not what I mean," I said. I opened the zipper on my bag and pulled out a T-shirt. "I brought along an extra shirt and pair of shorts just in case somebody forgot."

"That was smart," Kia said.

Right then Coach Barkley poked his head out the gym door. "Time," he called out loudly.

"Let's go," I mumbled. "And good luck to everybody."

We started in the door of the gym as parents and kids from the last squad started to file out. There were a lot more of them coming out than there were of us going in. Obviously their coach hadn't cut nearly as deep yet.

I followed Kia over to the corner bench where we both put down our bags.

"There are not many people here at all," Kia said.

I did a quick count. "Twenty-one kids. That means unless somebody is coming late he cut more than forty kids."

"That's a lot of cuts. Although more than the cuts, I'm surprised by some of the kids he *didn't* cut," Kia said.

"What do you mean?"

"Look who's over there in the corner."

I went to turn around when Kia grabbed my arm and jerked me back around.

"Try and be a little more casual, okay?" she asked.

Slowly I swiveled my head around. Just getting up from the bench was the player he'd been telling off at the end of the first try-out. I figured he was gone for sure after hearing that ... although I'd thought he'd done okay during the try-out.

The coach blew his whistle and the shrill sound echoed off the walls. We all ran to where he stood.

"Laps ... five half speed ... five full speed, then warm-ups," Coach Barkley barked. "I need somebody to lead the warm-ups. You," he said, pointing at me.

My eyes widened slightly in response.

"Can you do it?" he asked.

"I think I can."

"Think you can or know you can?" he demanded.

"I know," I said. "I've done it before."

"Good. You lead warm-ups after the laps. Now let's move it!"

Kia sprinted out to get to the front of the line and everybody fell in behind her.

As I ran I tried to picture what I'd do. Leading

the warm-ups meant that every eye — including the coach's — would be on me. I suddenly felt nervous and then instantly felt stupid for feeling nervous. I'd done warm-ups hundreds and hundreds of times and led them on at least a dozen occasions. Of course I could do warm-ups. I knew exactly what to do.

I turned my attention to the kids running laps with me. Nine of them were people I knew and knew well — kids I had played ball with before. A few of them, like D.J. and Jamie, and Brian and Mark, and of course Kia, had been my teammates for three straight years. I didn't spend my time focusing on any of them. Instead I looked at the kids I didn't know.

I remembered most of them from the first try-out. I recalled that a couple of them were really good. I tried to figure out which of them might be the coach's son. Nobody really looked like him at all, but there was one big kid who played like the coach would have played. He was all elbows and legs and hustle. He'd knocked me down twice last try-out — once during the warm-ups.

A few more were good — maybe as good as some of my friends. That meant that they had a chance of making the team and replacing somebody — maybe me.

Then there were three others who weren't quite so good. Two of them were the biggest kids in the gym. They were running at the very end, struggling to catch up to the rest of the line. At least I understood why they were still here. There's an old saying — you can't coach height. Maybe neither was even that good but they were tall and every team needed some height.

The final guy was more of a mystery. He was the one Kia and I had noticed — the guy the coach was chewing out at the end of the first try-out. He had a good shot and could dribble, but whenever I'd noticed him in that first try-out, he seemed to be going at half speed. I figured that was the kiss of death with this coach. I'd keep my eye on him. Who was I fooling ... I'd keep an eye on everybody

As we finished up the laps, I made my final decision on what I'd start with.

"Everybody in a circle," I called out.

A few of the kids started to slowly gather around.

"Was that an invitation or an order?" Coach Barkley asked.

"What?" I asked, not understanding what he meant.

"If you want people to listen to you, then take charge," he barked.

I nodded. "Hurry up!" I yelled loudly. "Let's get started!"

Everybody formed a circle and I started to lead them in a series of stretches. As I continued

with the warm-ups Coach Barkley slowly moved around the outside, watching everybody. I liked him watching the other kids because that meant his eyes weren't on me. Just then he looked up at me and our eyes met. He scowled and I looked away quickly.

★ ★ ★

"One minute for water!" Coach Barkley yelled out.

I dropped the ball and moved as quickly as my tired legs would carry me to my water bottle. Kia had already grabbed her water and was chugging it down.

"How much time left?" she asked.

"About twenty ... maybe twenty-five minutes," I panted out between swigs from my bottle.

"If his practices are going to be as hard as his try-outs it might be better not to make the team," Kia said.

"Don't even joke about that," I said. "Besides, *nothing* could be harder than this."

Kia held her water bottle upside down. "Do you have any more water?" she asked.

"None."

"I've got an extra."

It was that kid. I wasn't surprised he had water left because he wasn't sweating as hard as the rest of us.

"Thanks," Kia said as she took the bottle.

"L.B.," he said. "I'm L.B.," he said offering his hand.

"I'm Kia," she said, awkwardly shaking hands. "And this is Nick."

We shook hands as well.

"You two know how to play," he said.

"Thanks," Kia said. "You got a pretty good shot yourself."

"I get lucky sometimes."

Kia took a big gulp from the bottle and then flashed me a smile. "Let's get back before he calls us."

"That's smart," I said and put down my bottle. We trotted back. L.B. took another drink and didn't follow.

We reached Coach Barkley just as he blew the whistle. Kids started to reassemble.

"Hurry up, you're wasting my time!" he yelled angrily. "Anybody who needs more rest can have all the time they need ... after I cut them!"

That caused the last three stragglers, including L.B., to rush to his side.

"We're going to spend the last twenty minutes scrimmaging."

A rumble of excitement filled the gym.

"Before we get started, I have a question," Coach Barkley said.

Everybody perked up their ears.

"Raise your hand if you're tired."

Most of the kids put up a hand. I was tired but kept mine down. Maybe that was how he was going to pick the people to start.

"Those of you who didn't raise your hands obviously weren't working hard enough during practice, so I expect you to work hard during the scrimmage!" he bellowed.

I wished the floor could just open and swallow me up. He bent down and reached into an equipment bag at his feet. He pulled out a bunch of red and blue bibs — the pull-overs you use to determine which team you're on in a scrimmage. He started to toss them to kids. Kia got a red one ... so did D.J. ... Jamie got a blue one. Then he threw a blue one to me. He gave out five red and five blue. Getting them first was a good sign — it meant he knew we could play ball ... or did it mean that he thought we were on the edge and he needed to see us one more time before the cuts ... or maybe ... Oh, just stop thinking about it! I pulled the bib over my head.

"I have one last question before we get started," he said. "Do any of you have any friends here?"

"Sure," D.J. said. "Almost everybody."

"Yeah, lots of friends," Jamie added.

Most of the rest of us nodded our heads in agreement.

"Wrong," Coach Barkley said. "Completely and

utterly wrong. None of you have a single friend here."

Everybody looked confused.

"I see you don't believe me. Then let me ask this. Is there anybody here who'd give up a spot on their team for somebody else?"

Nobody answered. I looked down at the ground.

"That's what I figured. Lots of you know each other, been friendly, been teammates, but right now you shouldn't be thinking that anybody in this entire gym is your friend," he said waving his hand.

"Nobody, and I repeat, *nobody*, in here is your friend. Everybody, and I repeat, *everybody*, in here is your enemy. Their job is to beat you out of a spot on this team, to make you look like a fool. And if you don't treat them that way during this scrimmage, then you don't want to be on my team! Do you understand me?" he yelled, pointing at D.J.

"Yeah ... sure," he mumbled.

"How about you?" he asked, now pointing at another player.

"Yeah," he said.

Coach Barkley went from player to player asking each player if they understood, and each time he asked he yelled it out louder and louder until the gym walls seemed to be shaking.

"Now let's play some ball! I want to see some sweat and guts out there!"

Chapter Six

"Did you hear?" Kia yelled as she ran down the street toward me.

"Hear what?"

"Julian and Josh are gone."

My hands tightened on the basketball. "How do you know that?"

"I was talking to D.J. who was talking to Mark. He goes to school with Josh who told him about the two of them being called."

"That's awful," I said.

"But not unexpected."

"I guess it wasn't a complete surprise, but it's still too bad. Have you talked to them?" I asked.

"Not me. What would I say?"

"I don't know. Maybe that we're sorry, or something like that."

"You can call them if you want," Kia said, "but I really don't know what to say."

"I wonder how they're feeling?"

"How would you feel?" Kia asked.

"It makes me feel like I have to practice more before the next try-out," I said.

"Unless you're going to give up sleeping, I don't think you *can* practice anymore."

"I'll stop when I get my shot straightened out."

"Coach really has you spooked, doesn't he?" Kia said.

"And you're not afraid of him?" I asked.

"I don't know if that's the right word."

"Then what is?" I demanded.

"I don't know. He's ... he's ..."

"He's lots of things," I said. "At least he knows basketball."

"He does that, but he really can't play much anymore, can he?" she asked.

Instantly I knew what Kia was referring to. Just at the end of the last scrimmage he'd tried to demonstrate a proper lay-up and had come down badly on his ankle. He'd collapsed to the floor. He'd jumped back to his feet before anybody could say or do anything, but he was limping even worse then usual for the last few minutes before we left.

"My father showed me some of the *Sports Illustrated* articles about Coach Barkley," I said.

Kia scrunched up her face. "You mean from when he was playing?"

I nodded.

"Where would he get twenty-year-old issues of *Sports Illustrated*?" she asked.

"He has every issue for the past twenty-five years stored in boxes in our basement."

"You're joking, right?" Kia asked.

"Nope. He's says they'll be worth something some day," I explained. "My mother says she'll pay him something right now if he'll throw them all away."

"Can I see them?" Kia asked.

"You can, but are you sure you want to?"

"Why wouldn't I?"

"It's just that the more things I read about this guy the more worried I get," I said. "Are you sure you want to see them?"

"Nothing written twenty years ago is going to make much difference," she said. "I'm just curious."

"Come on in then and I'll show you."

Kia followed me into the house. I put my ball into a wicker basket sitting behind the door. That was one of the few shots I'd put in all afternoon.

"How many articles were about Mr. Barkley?" Kia asked.

"He's mentioned in a bunch of articles written about college basketball, but there's one whole article written about him and his injury."

"Let me see that one," Kia said.

I rummaged through the pile of magazines that were sitting on the coffee table.

"Here it is," I said, passing it to Kia.

She took the magazine and started scanning through the pages.

"It's in the back," I said.

She flipped through right to the very end and started to work back toward the front.

"*That* is gross!" Kia said loudly.

Without looking I knew what she had seen because I had the same reaction when I saw it the first time. It was the picture taken right after the injury. The coach was on the ground, a look of pure pain on his face, his foot pointing almost in the completely opposite direction. It looked as if it would fall right off if somebody just touched it.

"It's like you said," Kia said. "He's still holding onto the ball despite the pain. That's amazing."

"You want to know what's even more amazing?" I asked.

"What?"

"When this happened there was only two minutes left in the game."

"Yeah?"

"And the score was eighty-seven to forty-eight."

"For which team?" Kia asked.

"For Coach Barkley's team."

Kia looked at me hard. "So you're saying that they were up by thirty-nine points and he still was throwing himself around after a loose ball?"

I nodded my head.

"Then it didn't matter if he got the ball."

"Not at all. They were up by close to forty points and he was still hustling like the game was on the line."

Kia shook her head sadly. "You're right, that is amazing. I'm just not sure if it's amazingly stupid or not."

"What do you mean?"

"Just think," she said. "Instead of being on the bench, or just letting that ball go, he had to try and get it."

"And?"

"And that one loose ball cost him his whole career."

I let that sink in. Of course she was right. If only he'd turned it down a notch ... backed off a little. Then again, after seeing him run those two try-outs, I wasn't sure he even *could* turn it down.

Chapter Seven

I bounced the ball sharply three times and then spun it backward in my hands. All the time my eyes remained fixed on the hoop — not looking away like I was afraid if I did it might run away. I put up the foul shot — slight back-spin on the ball, good high arch, straight for the net and — it bounced off the rim and missed.

"Darn!"

"Nice try," Kia said as she scrambled after the rebound.

I'd missed more then half of my free throws at the end of the second try-out with the coach standing there watching. I'd been out here on my driveway every night since taking dozens and dozens of shots to try and get better. Instead I was getting worse.

"It was a good miss," Kia offered as she threw the ball back to me.

65

"There's no such thing as a good miss."

"Maybe not, but there sure are worse ways to miss," she said.

"What do you mean?"

"At least you hit the rim. It looked like it had a chance. It's a lot worse when it's an air ball. Remember that game last year when you had a chance to tie it up at the end and you put up an air ball?"

I shuddered at the memory. "As long as you're around I guess I never will get a chance to forget."

"Sorry," she apologized.

"I just wish I knew what I was doing wrong," I lamented.

"That's easy. You're thinking too much."

I gave her a questioning look.

"Don't think about it. Just do it."

"Great, I ask for advice and I get a TV commercial."

I looked at the hoop. Three bounces of the ball and a little spin, and then I shot. It missed the front of the rim.

Kia gobbled up the rebound. "Don't believe me if you don't want to, but you have to stop thinking and just let your mind go blank. That's what I do."

"Right. On the court ... in school ... at home."

Kia whipped the ball at my head. If I hadn't gotten my hands up fast, I would have caught it with my face.

"The foul shooting isn't doing me much good,"

I said. "Is there anything you want to practice or would that involve too much thought?"

She shrugged. "When you've reached perfection there isn't much left to improve on," she smirked. "But I have been giving one thing a lot of thought."

I instantly knew what she was thinking. It was the same thing that had cost me sleep last night.

"I keep thinking about Julian and Josh," she said. "Have you talked to them yet?"

I shook my head. "I was going to."

"Me too."

"But I still don't know what to say," I said.

"I know. No matter what you say it always sounds like you're rubbing it in," Kia said. "Sort of like we're still here and you're not."

"That could still change," I cautioned her. "Especially if I can't get my foul shots down."

"Don't be goofy. He's not going to cut you because you missed a couple of foul shots."

"He cut the two of them," I said.

"There were more than a few missed foul shots involved."

"Are you saying that you thought he should have cut them?" I asked.

"I didn't say that, but let's be honest," Kia said. "I know they're our friends, and we've been teammates for two years ... but ... you know," she said.

I didn't want to agree, but I couldn't really disagree with her unspoken words. I didn't want to say anything, but of all the players from last year's team they were probably the two weakest.

"He said he wouldn't be keeping everybody," she said.

"Wouldn't it have been better if he kept them a little bit longer before he cut them?"

"I don't know. If it were me, I'd rather know right up front and just get on with life."

I didn't even know if I could get on with life if I were cut. I'd never been cut from anything, not even something that wasn't important, and basketball was really important.

"Let's just hope we don't find out," I said. "Let's keep practicing."

I turned around, and without giving myself time to think, threw up a shot. It missed too.

"Hi, guys!"

I turned. "L.B.!"

He was standing at the end of my driveway. In his hand was a big black case.

"What are you doing here?" Kia asked.

"Walking home from music lessons. I just live a couple of blocks away."

"I didn't know that," I said.

"We just moved in a month ago," he said.

"This is my place."

"And I live a few blocks that way," Kia said,

pointing in the opposite direction.

"I have my piano lesson tonight," I said. "I don't understand why parents force their kids to take music."

"Nobody forced me to take them. It was my idea."

"You wanted to take music lessons?" I asked in disbelief.

He smiled. "I'm not taking music lessons. I'm taking *saxophone* lessons."

"Saxophone?" Kia asked.

"Alto sax," he said, patting the case. "Do you want to see it?"

"Sure … I guess," I said. What else were we supposed to say — 'no we don't want to see it'?

L.B. put down the case, undid the clasps, and opened it up. A shiny, brass saxophone nestled against the case's black, velvety lining.

He pulled out the big stem sort of part and then took out a second smaller piece. He fit them together. Next he pulled out another piece and fit it to the very top.

"Isn't it a beauty?" he asked.

Obviously he was very proud of it.

"It's nice looking," Kia said. "It looks complicated."

"It's like everything else. Once you know how to do it, there's no big trick."

"Are you any good?" Kia asked.

"Well …" he said and smiled. "You tell me."

L.B. put the saxophone to his lips and started to play.

"That's the *Pink Panther* theme!" I yelled.

L.B.'s eyes twinkled as he continued to play. He came to the end of the song and Kia and I cheered. He took a little bow.

"That was fantastic!" I said.

"How long have you been playing?" Kia asked.

"Almost two years."

"Two years? I've been playing the piano for almost four years and I'm not even close to that good," I said.

"Not even close," Kia agreed.

"Gee, thanks for your support," I said.

"What can I say?" she replied. "I call it like I see it. Or in this case like I hear it. You must practice a lot."

"At least an hour every day."

"That explains why you're so good," I said. "I practice for less then fifteen minutes and only when it doesn't get in the way of things like basketball."

L.B. chuckled. "That's funny, I'd practice more if it weren't for other things getting in the way. It looks like you two really love playing basketball," L.B. said.

"Sure ... don't you?" I asked.

"I like it fine, although I hate practices."

"But you don't mind practicing the saxophone," I said.

"That's different. Playing the saxophone is just having fun, you know, fooling around. Basketball practices are just work."

"Then you must not like these try-outs," Kia said.

"Hate 'em," he agreed. "How about you two?"

"Don't like them at all," Kia said.

"Me neither. It wouldn't be so bad if he didn't yell so much," I said.

"Actually ... I think he yells at you more than he does at anybody else," Kia said to L.B.

"No question there," L.B. agreed.

"We're still mad at him for cutting two of our friends," Kia said.

I nodded my head in agreement. "Josh and Julian were good guys and good players."

"Are *you* worried about making the team?" Kia asked.

L.B. got a serious look on his face as if he were really thinking his answer through.

"I worry ... but maybe not the way some other people worry."

"What do you mean?" Kia asked.

"Nothing, nothing at all."

"It's too bad our old coach had to leave. You would have liked him," I said.

"Yeah, he didn't yell or scream or anything," Kia added.

"I would have liked that better," L.B. agreed.

"But this guy does know the game," I said. "Did you know that he used to be a famous basketball player?"

"I know, but I just found that out last year."

"Last year? Why would you know last year?"

"My father said that me playing reminded him of his playing days, so he told me," L.B. continued.

A sick thought struck me square in the brain.

"Is the coach ... your ... your father?" I asked.

"I thought you knew," L.B. said.

"No, no, we didn't!" Kia answered.

"No, or we wouldn't have said the things we did," I blurted out. "I'm sorry, we didn't mean anything bad."

"Don't worry," L.B. said. "You didn't say anything that I didn't know or haven't thought myself. It's just sad that you two don't know him better, or at least know him differently."

"Differently?" Kia questioned.

"He's not like that all the time. He's usually so calm, and easygoing and funny and playful."

"Playful?" I asked, the word slipping out before I could even stop myself.

"Yeah, playful. It's just like something happens in the car on the way to the gym and he changes. And he's not himself again until a couple of hours after we're back home again."

"You're not going to tell him we said anything

are you?" Kia asked.

He shook his head and I felt a wave of relief wash over me.

"Thanks," Kia said. "Do you want to shoot a few hoops with us?"

"I appreciate the offer, but I better get ..." He paused. "Maybe just for a few minutes."

Chapter Eight

I dropped my bag to the ground and slumped down beside it.

"You okay?" Kia asked.

"Sure ... all of me except my mouth," I answered.

I poked my tongue into the cut inside my lower lip. I turned slightly to the side and spit out some blood on the sidewalk.

"Thanks for sharing that," Kia said.

"Sorry."

"Does it still hurt?"

"Not as bad as it did," I said.

"You took a good hit."

"There's no such thing as *taking* a good hit, only giving one."

"I think you impressed the coach," she said.

"And just how did me getting elbowed in the mouth impress him?"

"I don't think the elbow impressed him as

much as what you did after you got it."

"You mean bleeding and swelling up?"

"No, I mean getting the basket. You still made your shot."

"I did?"

"You didn't know?"

"I was sort of on the ground bleeding if you don't remember ... so I made the shot. I guess that's good."

"That was without a doubt the most brutal basketball I've ever been involved with," Kia said.

"It was awfully rough. The only thing that hurts more than my mouth are my legs and my ears."

"He's getting louder each week," Kia agreed. "By the way, where's your Dad?"

"I don't know ... it's not like him to be late," I said, scanning the parking lot for his car.

Instantly my mind started to whirl around all the possibilities from car crashes to alien abductions.

"He's okay, Nick," Kia said reassuringly. "Besides you're probably lucky he isn't here."

"How do you figure that?"

"Because if he were he might have been standing by the gym door waiting to get the coach's autograph."

For the second week in a row my father had been going on about wanting to get Coach Barkley's autograph and talk to him.

"You got a point there. That would be really

embarrassing … although I can't really blame him."

"You can't?"

I shook my head. "If Julius the Jewel Johnson was inside that gym right now where would you be?"

Kia smiled. "Standing right by the door ready to throw myself in front of him until I got his autograph."

"So you *do* understand."

"I guess so."

"Speaking of guesses," I said. "Any guess as to how well we did today?"

"Well … I did well," she joked. "And you didn't do badly yourself either. I think he even likes you."

"You do?" I asked in amazement.

"Think about it. He asked you to lead the warm-ups again, didn't he?"

"Yeah."

"And he didn't yell at you that much."

"Not that much," I admitted.

"Not as much as he yelled at almost everybody else. He really gave some people a hard time," Kia said.

He ripped a strip off half a dozen kids, the biggest strip coming off L.B.

"So you don't think we have anything to be worried about?" I asked hesitantly.

"Not a thing." She paused. "Not that that will stop you from worrying."

Of course she was right. Kia knew me really well — sometimes a lot better than I liked. But then again if you hang around with somebody every day for almost your entire life you'd have to expect that.

My mother had once said jokingly that the two of us were like an 'old married couple' who can complete each other's thoughts and sentences. I think she could tell by the look on my face that I wasn't very happy when she said that because she never repeated it.

It's hard enough having a girl as your best friend without your mother making cracks about it too. We got too much of that from other people already.

It was interesting that Coach Barkley hadn't said a word about Kia being a girl ... at least I hadn't heard him say anything. I wondered if he'd said something to Kia and she just hadn't mentioned it to me or —

"I do know some people who *should* be worried," Kia said, jarring me out of my thoughts.

I knew the kids she was talking about. It wasn't as if Coach Barkley was subtle when he wasn't happy about something.

"I think a couple of guys from last year's team are on thin ice," Kia continued.

I nodded my head in agreement. Both Greg and Ryan had looked lost out there. Unfortunately for them Coach Barkley had noticed and announced it repeatedly.

"Do you think he's going to cut Greg or Ryan?" Kia asked.

"I don't know anything for sure except that he sure does like to yell," I said.

"I don't think he could be quiet even if he wanted to," Kia continued.

"Can you imagine him in a library?" I asked.

"Sure," Kia said. "It would be something like this ... *Do you have any books?*" she bellowed. "*You know, tough books, hustling books, books that aren't afraid to hurl themselves off the shelves!*"

I started to laugh.

"Or just imagine him around the house, maybe talking about what he wants for breakfast," Kia laughed.

"Let me try this one," I said.

I paused and cleared my throat. "*I want eggs!*" I screamed, trying to make my voice sound deep. "*And I want them hard ... I don't want them runny ... I want them tough ... done on both sides ... I want that egg to feel the burn! Do you understand what I'm saying?*"

Kia practically fell off the curb laughing and —

"That *is* how I like my eggs," I heard a voice say from behind me.

My whole body felt a rush of electricity and I froze, the laughter stuck in my throat. Slowly,

ever so slowly, I turned around and looked up at Coach Barkley standing right behind us.

"And I do enjoy a good book every now and then," he continued. His voice was deep and his face unsmiling.

"I'm sorry ... we were just ... just ... " Kia stammered.

"Yeah ... we didn't mean to ..."

"I know what you were doing," he said. "You were making fun of your coach," he said, towering over of us.

We were dead. It didn't matter what we did anymore, we weren't going to make the team ... maybe we weren't going to live. He looked so big and angry and I was sure —

"And it's something I did to practically every coach I ever had in my entire life," he said, and his face suddenly and unexpectedly broke into a smile.

Wow, I didn't think he knew how to do that.

"You did?" I asked in amazement.

"Listen to this," he said. "*This past summer me and the little woman drove our motor home to the moon*," he said in a perfect imitation of Coach Riley.

"That was amazing!" I exclaimed.

He shrugged. "That's nothing. There was one coach I had in university who's voice I could do so well that I used to phone his wife and pretend

I was him," he said. "I'd call his home and ask her to make certain things for dinner or to tell her I'd be home late."

"You're joking!"

"Are you calling me a liar?" he asked, his face darkening just as quickly as he'd smiled.

"No, of course not!" I practically screamed.

"Good, because making fun of your coach isn't as bad as calling him a liar."

"I wasn't, I was just —"

"I'm just joking around with you now, so relax," he said.

"Oh, okay ... sure," I said, although being relaxed was the furthest thing from my mind.

"There was one big difference between what I did and what the two of you did, though," he said.

We both waited for him to continue.

"I wasn't stupid enough to do it when the coach was around to hear me," he said and started to chuckle.

"We won't do it again!" I protested.

"Sure you will," he argued. "Just be smart enough to do it somewhere I'm not. Understand?"

"Yes ... definitely ... of course," I stammered.

"Good. Do you two have a ride?" he asked.

"Yeah, my father is coming," I said.

"Is he usually late?"

"Never," Kia said. "It's not like him."

"Is he your father too?" Coach Barkley asked her.

"No, of course not!"

"I just thought the two of you might be twins or something."

"Us, twins?" I asked in amazement.

"We don't even look anything alike," I said.

"Neither do I and my twin sister."

"You have a twin sister?" Kia asked in amazement.

"Her name is Laura. When we were your age we spent all our time together."

"Did she play basketball too?" Kia asked.

"Great little player. Up until the age of about ten she could beat me more than half the time when we played one on one."

"She could beat you?" I asked in amazement.

"Don't sound so surprised," he said. "I bet Kia can take you a lot of the time."

"Well ..."

"We're pretty even," Kia said. "Did your sister keep on playing basketball?"

"Right through high school and into university. She was a good player. Better than half the kids on my high school team."

"So you two played on the same team in high school too?" Kia asked.

"Nope she played on the girls' team. Back then girls weren't allowed to play with the boys no matter how good they were."

"That's stupid," Kia snapped.

"Of course, that's how we feel now, but back then nobody thought much about it one way or another. It was just the way it was. Besides, you'd be amazed at how many people still feel that way today."

"But you don't, right?" Kia asked.

"If I did, do you think you'd still be here?" Coach Barkley asked.

"I guess not. Does your sister still play?" Kia asked.

"I think she plays one night a week, but she's pretty busy with her kids ... she has four of them."

"That would keep her busy."

"But she still loves the game." He paused. "You know I won't ever have any problem with a girl being on any team I coach."

I could almost *feel* Kia smile without even looking at her.

"But I also have no problem cutting her if she isn't good enough and isn't tough enough," he continued.

Just like I could feel her smile, I could almost hear Kia swallow when he finished the sentence.

"So you two are just friends," Coach Barkley said.

I was going to answer when I remembered what he said about not having any friends and hesitated.

"It's okay to be friends outside the try-outs," he said.

"We're best friends," Kia said.

"Anybody ever hassle you about hanging out together?" he asked.

"Sometimes," I admitted.

He nodded his head. "Me and my sister used to get that all the time. Speaking of family, you two know my son," he said gesturing to the side.

L.B. was standing just off to the side.

"Yep. We even played some ball together on the driveway at my house a couple of days ago," I said.

"On my way back from saxophone lessons," L.B. added.

"He even played the saxophone for us," Kia said.

"That's not surprising. He's always willing to practice some things," Coach Barkley said.

L.B. turned to his father. "Speaking of practice we better get going or I'll be late." He turned to us. "I have a saxophone lesson."

"But I thought your lessons were on Wednesday?" Kia asked.

"I have them twice a week."

"We'll get there on time, don't worry," Coach Barkley said. "Are you two okay if we leave you here?"

"No problem, I'm sure my father won't be any

more than a few — there he is!" I yelled as I saw his car pull up to the curb just down from us.

"We'll see you two next week," Coach Barkley said.

"Next week?" I questioned. "Does that mean we … that we …"

"Made the next cut?" he asked.

I nodded my head.

"Neither of you has anything to worry about. At least for *this* week."

Chapter Nine

We rushed up to meet my father. Part of the reason I wanted to hurry was to avoid him coming up and talking to Coach Barkley. Kia and I jumped into the back seat.

"Was that who I thought it was?" he asked before we could even close the door.

"Depends who you think it is?" I asked.

"Len Barkley, of course," he said, staring out the windshield as the coach and his son walked in the other direction.

"Then you thought right. But aren't you more interested in how the try-outs went and how we did, or why my lip is all swollen?" I asked.

"Your lip?" he questioned, quickly turning around to look at me. "How did that happen?"

"I caught an elbow."

"Did you have your mouth guard in?"

"If I didn't I'd be carrying my front teeth in

my bag instead of my mouth," I said.

"I guess that's part of the game," Dad said. "Accidents happen."

"Lots of them," Kia said.

"Besides me there was a bleeding nose and I bet everybody has some bruises and bumps."

"I thought there was going to be a fist fight at one point," Kia said.

"It was very rough," I agreed.

"That's no surprise if Len Barkley coaches the way he played. He didn't believe in taking any prisoners."

"That sounds about right," I said, "because if we keep getting that many injuries nobody is going to survive the try-outs to make the team."

"Well, at least we survived for another week," Kia said.

"He told us we made the next cut," I explained to my father.

"That's great news! You must both be very happy!"

"I'll be happier when my lip stops hurting."

"Bumps and bruises you get over. Some things stay with you for life," he said.

"Things like broken bones?" I asked.

"No, things like making a great play, or being part of a team, or playing for a certain coach, or winning a game."

"Or playing against a great player?" I asked.

"Exactly!" my father said. "You two may think this

is stupid, but I remember getting ready for that game against your coach. I remember all the things I'd heard about him and I was scared to go out there."

"I believe it."

"So do I," Kia agreed. "It's scary enough just having him yell out instructions to us."

"He yells a lot," I agreed.

"So he's pretty tough," my father said.

"Yes, and no," I answered. "He seemed pretty nice when we were talking to him just now."

"Yeah, he did," Kia agreed. "He was even joking around and telling us stories."

"Was that his son with him?" my father asked.

"Yeah. His name is Len too, although he goes by L.B.," Kia answered.

"Named after his old man. Does he play like him too?"

"Not really."

"You mean he isn't good?"

"It's not that he isn't good," I said. "He's just different."

"Almost gentle," Kia said.

"Gentle? What does that mean?" my father asked.

"I don't know, maybe I'm not using the right word."

"No, I hadn't thought about it but when you use that word it seems right to me too," I said.

"So how is a basketball player gentle?" my father asked again.

"He doesn't go underneath the hoop very much," Kia explained.

"I don't think he does at all," I agreed. "He plays on the outside. He's got a nice shot, though."

"And he's smart with the ball," Kia continued.

"And a good passer as well," I said.

"But he doesn't seem to like it when things get rough," Kia added.

"He just isn't really very intense. You remember that one loose ball when —"

"He could have dove and got it and he didn't," Kia said, finishing my sentence.

"Exactly. The coach blew down the play and started yelling at him so loud I thought he was going to peel the paint off the key."

"That doesn't surprise me. The guy was a fanatic for people not trying," my father said. "I remember watching one of his games on TV when he practically got into a fist fight with one of his own teammates because the guy was dogging it."

"Yeah, but it's different when it's your own kid ... you know, yelling at him like that in front of everybody."

"That surprises me even less. People are always hardest on their own kids."

"They are?" I asked.

"Definitely. Especially when the kid is doing something that the parent was good at. Think about how your mother reacted when you got that 'B' in writing for second term last year."

I shuddered. I'd always got top marks in writing and when your mother is a professional writer it's supposed to be that way. She didn't exactly get mad at me, but I remember her saying how 'disappointed' she was in my marks. I would have preferred if she had yelled. Then for the whole third term she was always asking me about assignments and looking at the rough copies of my stories and making me read things and generally being a real pain.

"And speaking of your mother," my father said. "How about if we don't talk much about —"

"How rough things have been," I said, cutting him off.

"Exactly. I'm not saying that we should lie to her or anything. I just think it would be better not to get her all worked up, that's all."

"I can agree with that," I said.

"Good. I always knew you were a smart kid ... even when you got a 'B' in writing."

Chapter Ten

"I'll get it!" I yelled as I ran for the phone.

"Hello," I said into the receiver.

"Is this Nick?"

My heart leaped into my throat as I recognized the voice. It was Coach Barkley and the only reason he could be calling was to tell me that I was cut from the team, but he told me and Kia that we were okay for another week so he couldn't be calling to —

"Hello, are you still there?" he asked.

"Yes … yes I am, and this is Nick."

"This is Mr. Barkley calling. How's your lip?"

"It's good, it's fine, no problem, good," I stammered, sounding like an idiot.

"Glad to hear that."

"You called to ask about my lip?" I asked, hoping that was the only reason he was calling.

He started to laugh. "No, I'm calling because

I've arranged an exhibition game at the college for this Thursday night."

"A game ... you mean you've picked the team?"

"Not yet. The game will help me decide who will be on the team. Can you make it?"

"Yeah, sure."

"Excellent. Wear a white T-shirt to the gym. Game starts at seven so I want you there at six-thirty at the latest."

"I can be there at six."

"Six-thirty will be fine," he said. "And let your parents know that they're welcome to come and watch if they want."

"They can?"

"Parents are always welcome for games. It's practices and try-outs when I want them far away. See you Thursday."

"Thanks ... sure ... bye," I said as I put down the phone.

"Who was that?" mom asked.

"It was the coach. He called to say there's a game Thursday night."

"What time?"

"Seven, so we have to be there at six-thirty."

"But you have a piano lesson at six-thirty."

"I can't make it," I said. "Can't we reschedule it?"

She shook her head. "We can, but once, just once, I'd like it if a basketball game had to be rescheduled because of piano."

"Come on, Mom, be reasonable."

"I am being reasonable. Matter of fact I have a very reasonable suggestion. Since you won't be going to piano, you should double up your practice tonight."

I opened my mouth to protest but thought better of it.

"Sure, Mom, no problem," I said as I trotted off to start piano.

★ ★ ★

"They're huge!" Kia hissed at me as she fell in behind me in the line.

We were going through our pre-game warm-ups. Both of us had one eye on our warm-ups and the other eye trained on our opponents at the other end doing their warm-ups.

"They can't be our age," Kia continued.

"They're not," I confirmed. "I heard some of the parents talking. They're two years older than us."

"Then why are we playing them?" D.J. asked as he filed in behind Kia.

"Outlet!" I screamed as the man under the basket grabbed the ball and fired it to me. I fed the ball to the player charging from the other line and then trotted to join the next line. Kia did the same thing and fell into the line behind me again.

"D.J.'s got a good question. Why are we playing these guys?" Kia asked.

"I guess he figures it'll be a good test or something."

"A test of what, how much we can lose by?" Kia asked.

"Just because they're bigger and older doesn't mean they're better than us," I said.

"Since when have you become such a positive thinker?" she asked.

"The bigger they are, the harder they fall," I said.

"Great, now you're quoting bumper stickers," Kia said. "Besides the way I heard it was something like, the bigger they are, the harder they fall on top of you."

"Funny."

"It won't be when they land on you. Look at the size of that one guy," she said, pointing to a player warming up at the far end. "He's bigger than my mom's car."

I looked away and up to the stands. Both my parents, along with Kia's mother, were sitting alongside other parents and brothers and sisters and assorted people I didn't know.

"Big crowd," Kia said.

"Bigger than we usually have for a game, especially an exhibition game," I agreed.

"I think that's because Coach Barkley doesn't

allow parents at the try-outs, so everybody is curious about what we're like."

"That makes sense," I said. "Although if there are other parents like my father, they're coming here to look at the coach as much as they've come to see us play."

"You're not kidding. I heard a couple of the parents talking about him. You'd think he was some sort of famous singer instead of a guy who played basketball twenty years ago," Kia noted.

Just then Coach Barkley waved to call us in. Everybody on the floor rushed to his side. The last to get there, as always, was L.B.

"I'm going to be playing everybody fairly equally throughout the game," Coach Barkley said. "I want to see how all of you do in game situations."

He'd already told me that I was one of the players who were starting. That was a good sign — at least I was pretty sure it was.

"There are sixteen of you left," Coach Barkley continued. "By the end of this game I'm going to know which are my twelve and which four walk out the door."

He wasn't saying anything I didn't already know. I figured this game was really the last try-out.

"Does anybody know what a 'practice player' is?" Coach Barkley asked.

One of the new guys raised his hand. "A player who likes to practice?"

"Nobody likes to practice," Coach Barkley smirked. "It's somebody who's a world-beater during practices but has nothing to give during a game. Try-outs are the same thing. Lots of people can look good in drills or little scrimmages, but don't have the goods when it's game time. Right now is game time. Everybody here want to make the team?" he asked.

There was a rumbling of 'sure' and 'yes' and nodding of heads.

"I can't hear you!" he yelled.

"Yes!" I screamed back along with everybody else.

"Then show me! Show me that you want it!" he growled.

Almost like on cue everybody started to howl and scream and cheer.

"I want to see who's got the heart and guts to be on my squad!"

Again, the entire huddle of kids cheered — well almost the entire huddle. L.B. was silent and there was a look on his face ... it was hard to describe. He looked as if maybe he'd bitten down on something sour.

"Now let's play ball!"

I walked out onto the court and looked for my match-up. He wasn't hard to find. Just like everybody on the other team he was bigger than me. He smirked as I moved in beside him. I moved

96

into position for the tip-off and the player stepped into me, pushing me over to the side.

"You going to take that from him?" I heard Coach Barkley howl.

I looked over. He was staring directly at me. I lowered my shoulder and pushed back — hard. He didn't move much but reacted by bumping me with his hip and —

"Both of you settle down or we'll start the game with the two of you having a technical foul," the ref warned.

We both moved slightly to the side, allowing a little bit of space between us.

"You'll be paying for that," the player said under his breath.

I figured I probably would, but, if I hadn't done it, I would have been paying for it in a much more painful way. He didn't scare me nearly as much as the coach did.

I looked at our center standing beside their number five man. There was no way in the world we were going to get this tip. Instead what I had to do was figure out where it was going to go. Was their center going to tip it back to set up a play or try to tip it forward — over my head — to try for an early fast break basket? I knew what I'd try if I were doing it.

I took a deep breath and waited as the ref went to toss up the ball. Just as he started to throw it into the air I jumped away from the circle. My man tripped over me, falling to the ground as the ball soared up and then was tipped right toward me! I grabbed the ball and quickly fed it up to Kia. She stopped, set, and put up a shot ... it dropped!

At least we weren't going to be shut out I thought as the bench and bleachers went wild.

"Press!" yelled out Coach Barkley. "Zone press!"

The coach had had us work on the press for the last part of the last practice and had warned us we'd need to know it soon enough.

We all tried to scramble into our places, but before we could set up they threw the ball in and broke the press up the side. A fast pass went up to a breaking man and the score was tied.

"Time out!" screamed Coach Barkley.

We trotted over to the bench.

"What sort of a press was that?" he bellowed. "That stunk! You got beat and you didn't even have the guts to run back up the court when they beat you! Next five into the game."

"What?" Kia asked in disbelief.

"The five of you on the bench! And if I hear one more word you're on the bench for the rest of the game!"

I felt like somebody had punched me in the side of the head. I staggered over to the bench and sat down. I couldn't believe I'd been benched

... that all of us had been benched. The game was less then thirty seconds old and I was sitting on the bench!

I lowered my eyes to the ground. The last thing I wanted to see were my parents sitting there looking at me. I'd never been benched before in my entire life, and they were sitting up there watching it happen. What would they think?

★ ★ ★

The buzzer went ending the first half. The score read 36 to 24. I didn't care about the score. I didn't care about anything except that I wanted to get through this nightmare.

Coach Barkley muttered something under his breath, tossed down a water bottle, and then stomped across the floor toward the dressing room. All of us sat on, or stood by the bench, not following.

"That was unbelievable," Kia said. "He must have benched everybody at least twice."

She was right about that. I thought the only reason I or anybody else got a chance to go back out was because he kept getting mad at somebody new. It was like we all took turns being yelled at and benched. And when he wasn't yelling at us he was yelling at the other team's players, or their coach or the refs. There were times it seemed like his eyes glazed over and he was so mad he was practically spitting when he yelled. I'd never heard anybody carry on like that before — ever — anywhere. It was like watching a madman.

L.B. got up slowly from the bench and started across the floor after his father. Reluctantly other kids began to trail after him. I staggered to my feet and followed along, although it felt like my feet were filled with lead. I didn't want to go into that dressing room. I just wanted to leave — change out of my basketball shoes and go home.

The coach was pacing back and forth as we filed in, trying not to make a sound, and slumped down onto the benches.

"Don't any of you want to win?" Coach Barkley asked.

There was silence.

"Are you all deaf as well? Doesn't anybody here want to win? It looked like none of you were even trying out there."

"We tried," L.B. said so quietly I could hardly hear him and he was sitting right beside me.

"What did you say?" Coach Barkley questioned.

L.B. looked up at his father. "I said we tried."

"Not hard enough!" Coach Barkley stated. His voice had gotten louder with each word. "Those kids in that other dressing room tried."

"They're older than we are," L.B. said.

I had to hand it to him. I didn't want to say anything.

"That's nothing but an excuse! I don't want any excuse!"

I could hear him getting louder and he started to pace faster around the room.

"You all just died and the reason you died is because none of you, not one, has enough heart!" he yelled, looking right at his son. "You're acting like losers and I don't want any losers on my team! Do you know what a loser is?" he demanded.

I kept my eyes focused squarely on the floor.

"A loser is somebody who stops trying to win. Is there anybody in here who thinks he's lost already?"

There was no answer. We all just sat there and said nothing.

"Do you think we can win?" he demanded, pointing at one kid.

"Um … maybe … I guess."

"You guess! If you don't think we can win, maybe you better just pack your things and go home now!" he bellowed. "Do you think we can win?" he demanded of him again.

"Yes … yes, I think we can win," he stammered.

"Because if any of you don't think you can win, then maybe I'm going to have to cut everybody in this room and start fresh with those kids

I've already cut! Maybe some of them don't have as many skills as this bunch, but they certainly have to have more heart! You all have the last half of this game to prove something to me ... and if you don't ... don't any of you expect to be on *my* team."

Chapter Eleven

"Are you okay?" my mother asked as she went to put an arm around my shoulder.

"I'm fine," I mumbled as I slipped past her. "I just want to get to the car and go home."

I felt like I was close to tears and the last thing I wanted was to cry in front of everybody. I stumbled out the door, down the steps, and toward where we parked the car. I could hear my mother behind me.

"Nick, wait up," she called out.

I slowed down but didn't stop. She came up beside me.

"You're limping."

"A little." I'd been landed on going for a loose ball. My first thought was about what had happened to the coach twenty years before. I was so relieved when I got up with just a limp.

"Your team really played well."

"We lost."

"But you almost came back there in the second half."

"All that matters is that we lost."

"Is that what your coach said?" she asked icily.

"He didn't say much after the game," I said.

"Maybe he didn't have any voice left after all that yelling he did *during* the game," she said.

I stopped at the back door of the car and waited as she opened her side and hit the door release allowing me in. I threw my bag in and climbed in after it.

My father was nowhere to be seen. I wondered where he was. My mother climbed into the front seat and started the car.

"Where's Dad?" I asked.

"Your father won't be too long, I hope," she said.

I slumped farther down in the seat. I didn't want to see anybody and I didn't want to talk to anybody.

"Here he comes," my mother said.

My father climbed into the passenger seat.

"Did you talk to him?" she asked.

"Talk to who?" I asked.

"The coach," my mother said.

"Why did you want to talk to him?" I asked. Was he going to tell him off for benching me? It wasn't like I didn't deserve it … I guess.

"We both thought that somebody should talk

to him," my mother said.

"About what?" I questioned, getting more anxious by the second.

"About what I saw in the game. That was the most disgusting thing I've ever seen in my entire life!" my mother said shaking her head angrily.

"I'm sorry ... we didn't lose by that much ... I tried as hard as I could ... I didn't mean to disappoint everybody," I sputtered, trying as hard as I could to fight back the tears.

"It was a good game. You played well," my father protested. "Coming back and only losing by four points to a team that much older is a victory."

We'd all played much better — especially L.B. His outside shooting was a big part of the reason we'd gotten so close. If only I could have done more.

"I didn't mean to get benched ... I just kept screwing up, and I'm really sorry I let everybody down," I blabbered and the tears started to flow.

My mother reached over the seat and grabbed my hand. "Nicky, I'm not upset about *you*. It's that ... that, *man* ... that supposed coach!"

"The coach?"

"Yelling and screaming and ranting and raving! He was going on like the world was at stake instead of some basketball game!"

"He really was into the game, wasn't he?" my

father said with a laugh.

"Into the game?" my mother said in disbelief. "Is that what you call it?"

"He coaches like he used to play, with all his heart," my father said. "Did you see the way he brought them back and forced everybody on the team to play so well? That man really knows basketball."

"But what did he say when you talked to him?" my mother asked.

"It was hard to talk because there were so many people around. He said that they could have played better."

"But didn't you go over to talk to him about how he acted?" my mother asked, sounding confused.

"No ... I just wanted to ask him when he'd be making his final decision about who was on the team."

"You mean you didn't say anything about his behavior ... about yelling at everybody, including our son?"

My father shrugged. "Is that what you wanted me to talk to him about?" Now my father sounded confused.

"Of course! Isn't that what you wanted to say to him?"

"I just wanted to talk about the game ... how the kids did ... how Nick did. You know, things like that. Basketball things."

"I don't care about any of those things," my mother protested. "All I know is that he isn't a very nice man. And I don't think I want my son playing for a man like that."

"You don't want him to do what?" my father asked in disbelief.

I straightened up in the seat. What was she saying?

"You heard me. I don't think we should let our son have anything to do with that man. Look at him," she said, pointing at me. "He's in tears!"

"He's in tears because he thought you were mad at him!"

"That wasn't the reason and —" my mother suddenly stopped. "I think that it would be best if we talked about this later ... by ourselves ... after Nick goes to bed."

"I think that *would* be better," my father agreed.

A deep, heavy silence suddenly filled the car. I was grateful that they weren't arguing, but scared of what they'd be saying when they started again. The strangest thing was that I wasn't even one hundred percent certain who I wanted to win the argument.

★ ★ ★

I waited in bed for ten minutes before making my move. I figured they'd start to talk about things soon, if they hadn't already began. Ever since we'd gotten home they'd both been talking about other things. Talking really politely and calmly about things that I knew neither wanted to talk about. They were just waiting for me to go to bed so they could start discussing things.

I climbed out of bed and crept to the door. I could just barely hear voices. I couldn't tell what they were talking about. If they were talking about my basketball future, they were doing it very quietly. They hardly ever fought and when they did it usually wasn't very long or loud. There were only a couple of times I'd heard them get as angry as they had during the car drive home tonight.

There wasn't much point in even trying to listen from my bedroom door. I might as well go back to bed ... or get closer. I moved from my door to the top of the stairs. I could hear them more clearly, but not enough to make out exactly what they were saying, so —

"It's just basketball!" my mother said loudly, her voice suddenly becoming audible.

My father's voice answered back, but I couldn't make out any of his words. I needed to get closer now that I knew for sure that I was the topic of their conversation.

I took a tentative step down the first stair. I moved slowly. Down the second and then the third and the fourth steps. Then I was struck by the thought of what would happen to me if they caught me eavesdropping on them?

I'd be in big trouble ... unless I told them they had woken me up with their loud conversation. Then they'd feel too guilty to get mad at me. Reassured I started down again. I stopped at the bottom of the stairs.

"I've never complained about him playing so much basketball," my mother stated loudly.

"Hah! Of course you have!" my father replied, and he was right — she did complain about me playing ball too much.

"Well, maybe I've said a word or two, but I've never *stopped* him from playing."

Now it was her turn to be right. She never had stood in my way. She complained about it but she was always there to drive me to and from places, and to cheer me on, and to bring out drinks for me and my friends when we were playing on the driveway. She was even starting to understand the game.

"Then why are you trying to stop him now?" my father asked.

"Do I really have to go through this again? Don't you know?" she questioned.

"I just want to make sure I fully understand your objections, that's all," my father replied.

"Fine. It's simple. I object to that man. You saw the way he was carrying on and heard the

110

things he said."

"I heard him yelling, but he was just being intense. Basketball is an emotional game," my father argued.

"But it's only a game. Nothing that happens out there is life and death!"

"It's not life and death, but it is important. If you'd ever played the game you'd know," my father tried to explain.

"I've never done lots of things, but that doesn't mean I don't know what's right and what's wrong."

"But if you'd ever played, or even ever dreamed about the game, you'd know what a wonderful opportunity it is for Nick to play under this coach."

"A wonderful opportunity for what? To be brow-beaten, yelled at, and humiliated?"

"Of course not. An opportunity to learn about basketball. A season under this coach could elevate his game to a whole new level," he said. "Didn't you see how excited he was tonight?"

"I don't know if that was excitement or fear."

Fear ... that was what I was feeling out there a lot during the game. Fear of losing, fear of making a mistake, fear of the other team ... and fear of the coach and what he'd say.

"You saw how upset he was after the game," my mother continued.

"It's all right to be upset when things don't go right," my father argued. "Besides it's not like he couldn't use a little toughening up."

Toughening up ... what did he mean by that? Didn't he think I was tough enough?

"We're talking about our son, not a piece of leather. Besides, if we're not careful you'll kill his love of the game."

"That'll never happen. He loves playing basketball," my father protested.

"I wonder if he still will after playing a season with that man? How many times have you seen him out on the driveway playing basketball the last two weeks?"

"He's been out there practicing a lot," my father answered, and he was right, I was out every night.

"I didn't say practicing, I said playing."

"What do you mean?" my father asked.

"I mean out there, either by himself or with Kia or other kids, just fooling around playing basketball, having fun."

"Well ..."

"He doesn't play anymore. He's just standing out there practicing his free throws, or his fade in shots or —"

"Fade *away* shots," my father said interrupting her.

"I don't care what they're called. All I know is that it's supposed to be fun and it looks like work."

"He's just trying to be the best he can be. Would you be arguing if he were spending this much time on his homework or on writing stories?"

"That's different," my mother countered.

"I don't think it is," he said. "He's trying to be the best he can, and this coach can help him reach his potential. If I'd had somebody like that when I was a kid, there's no telling how far I could have —"

"Is that what this is all about?" my mother demanded.

"Is that what all what is about?"

"You think it's right for Nick because you think that's what you would have liked to have happen to you when you were a kid."

"Of course, I would have loved to have had somebody like Len Barkley be my coach when I was young. Who wouldn't want that?"

"I wouldn't want that," she said.

"Hah! Then maybe this isn't about what *I* want, but what *you* want!"

"Me?"

"Yes. Because you wouldn't want to have somebody handle you like that, you don't think that it's right for Nick either."

"That's not it at all!" she stated loudly. "I'm offended that you'd even suggest that!"

"And how is that different from you accusing me?" my father demanded.

"Well … well … well …" my mother stammered.

I waited for her to continue. And waited. And

waited. There wasn't a sound. Why weren't they talking? Were they that angry that they weren't even going to talk any more? If I didn't like them fighting, I really didn't like the silence of them not fighting.

"I'm sorry," my father said. "I didn't mean to get you so upset."

"I'm sorry too," my mother answered. "I didn't mean anything by what I said ... honestly ... I'm just worried about Nick."

"I know you're worried. And I understand why. I really can see both sides," my father said.

"So can I. I know how much both of you love basketball."

"About the only thing I don't know is how we're going to resolve this," he said.

There was more silence.

"Maybe we should just be getting to bed," my father said. "It's getting late. Maybe if we get a good night's sleep, we can figure what to do tomorrow. We can at least talk about it tomorrow."

"I wonder if it would help if we asked Nick to be part of this discussion?" my mother said.

Now there was something I didn't like even more than them making the decision for me. Did they expect me to choose who I was going to agree with and who I was going to disappoint?

"It makes sense for Nick to have input into something this important," my father agreed.

"Tomorrow night we'll all sit down and try to come to some sort of agreement. Now let's get to bed."

I turned and silently scampered up the stairs before they could discover me. I slipped in my door and pulled it almost completely closed after me. I climbed into bed and pulled the covers up all the way over my head.

I started to think. Would it be better for them to make the decision or for me to make the decision? I tried to imagine what it would be like not to play basketball. Then I tried to think how it would be to spend an entire season playing for Coach Barkley. Maybe it would be better if they made the decision for me. At least that way I'd have somebody to blame.

Chapter Twelve

"Thank you for the very good supper … may I be excused?" I asked as I grabbed my plate and glass and got up from the table.

"You're welcome," my mother said. "But before you leave, we wanted to talk for a while."

This was what I was waiting for — and dreading — all day. I'd hoped that if I could get away fast, they'd forget all about having our conversation.

"Could it wait for later? I have a lot of homework to do."

I really didn't have much to do, but I was prepared to spend most of the night in my room at least pretending to do homework if it meant getting out of the discussion I knew was coming. I'd already spent far too much time thinking about how this might go.

"It won't take long," my father offered. "Come on and sit back down for a while."

I put my dishes on the counter and reluctantly returned to the table.

"You remember that discussion your mother and I had in the car last night about you playing basketball?" my father began.

"Yeah ... sure I remember something about it," I offered.

"Well, we want to talk to you about basketball," my mother said.

"What about basketball?" I asked, feigning innocence.

"About the try-outs," my father answered. "How it's going and what you think about it. Things like that."

"It's going okay, I guess."

"And are you enjoying it?" my mother asked.

"No," I said, shaking my head.

My mother looked at my father and gave him an 'I told you so' look.

"But I never enjoy try-outs. I'm always worried about how things are going to turn out. You know that."

"Of course. What I meant is are you more worried about it this time than you were the last time?" she asked.

"Yeah, I am, but that has to do with the new coach," I said.

"Is there something he's doing that makes you more worried?" my mother asked.

"He's pretty tough, but maybe it's just that any new coach would have made me more nervous."

"But it is kind of cool to have a former basketball star as your coach, isn't it?" my father asked.

"It's okay."

"And I bet he really, really knows the game," my father continued.

I nodded my head in agreement. There was no way anybody could argue with that. I'd learned things from him already in the try-outs and I was sure he'd have lots and lots of things to teach those people who made the team.

"He certainly got a lot out of you and all your teammates during that game," my father added.

It was clear what was going on here. Maybe my mother and father hadn't agreed what would happen, but that hadn't changed how they both felt. And now they were trying to get me to support their side.

"That game last night was part of what we wanted to discuss," my mother said. "What did you think of the game?"

"I would have liked to have won."

"Besides that. Were you okay with the way your coach acted?"

"Acted?" I asked, pretending I didn't know what she meant. I was spending most of this conversation pretending one thing or another.

"The way he screams all the time," she explained.

"He doesn't scream all the time."

"But he does scream a lot more than your last coach."

"Or any other coach I've ever had," I admitted.

The corner of my mother's mouth curved slightly into the beginning of a smile.

"And how about when he yells at you?" she continued.

"Sometimes he has to yell to get people's attention in the gym. There's a lot of noise with the balls and people talking and the crowd making noise," I said.

"So it doesn't bother you?" she asked, sounding confused.

"I don't like it. I don't like it when you or Dad yell at me either."

"Come on, Nick, we hardly ever raise our voices."

"Hardly ever," I muttered under my breath, thinking back to last night when I'd heard a lot of raised voices.

"Your mother and I spent some time discussing things about you and this basketball team last night."

"You did?"

"You knew that," my mother said.

I swallowed hard. Had they seen me listening or somehow —

"We told you last night in the car that we'd continue to talk after you went to bed," she said.

"Oh, yeah, that's right," I said, feeling relieved. "I just didn't know if you did, that's all."

"In fact we talked quite a while," my father said.

"And we were wondering if it was something that you really wanted," my mother added.

"You mean being on the team?" I asked.

"I ... we ... have some concerns about your being part of the team."

"What do you mean 'concerns'?" I asked.

"About your coach and his attitude," my mother answered.

"Not all of his attitude. We know that basketball is an emotional game, and sometimes you have to get into the game even when you're on the bench," my father added.

"We just wanted to get your opinion about everything," my mother said.

"About being on the team?" I asked again.

My mother nodded.

I shrugged. "What's there to think about? I don't even know if I'm going to make the cut."

"And if you do?" my mother asked.

I shrugged again. "Then I'm on the team."

"And that's what you want ... right, Nick?" my father asked.

"Sure ... of course."

"And if you couldn't be part of the team, would that be all right?" my mother asked.

"I guess I'd play house league basketball or ..."

I paused. Had they made a decision after I went to bed that I couldn't be part of the team even if I were offered a spot? Were they just pretending that they wanted my opinion when they'd already made the decision for me?

I felt a rush of anger. "Are you saying I can't be part of the team?"

Nobody said a word. My mother just looked worried.

"Mom?" I asked.

She took a deep breath. "I have some reservations about your being part of any team coached by that man, but your father and I came to an agreement today. Our agreement is that the person who has to make the decision is you."

"Me?" I asked.

"That's right," my father said. "Whether you want to be part of this team or don't is up to you."

"Maybe we won't be completely happy with any decision you make," my mother added. "But we'll support you whether you play or not."

"Thanks," I said.

"And you're okay with that … right?" my father asked.

I nodded my head. That meant that if I were offered a spot on the team I was free to take it. It sounded like my father had won the argument, even though they had come to some sort of agreement.

My father knew that there was no way I'd turn down the chance to play basketball if I were offered a spot on the team. I'd just grab that spot and ... suddenly I had a strange feeling right in the pit of my stomach.

"Now that we're finished, you might want to get up to your room and start on all that home-work," my father said.

"Yeah, I guess I better."

I walked out of the kitchen thinking about how none of this was particularly fair. I had to go and pretend to do homework I didn't have, and it still hadn't got me out of that conversa-tion. Well, at least they were letting me make the choice to be part of the team. Strange ... I guess I wanted to be the one who made the decision ... free to choose to be on the team. Because I definitely wanted to be on the team. At least I was pretty sure I did.

Chapter Thirteen

We all stood outside the door of the gym, waiting for it to open and for us to be let in. There was a lot of talking and joking around, but I could tell everybody was nervous. Really nervous. Even Kia had been pretty quiet on the drive over.

I stood off to the side and watched. I didn't feel that anxious. That was even stranger than Kia being nervous. I always felt on pins and needles, but now I didn't. One thought kept rolling around in my head — what was the worst that could happen? Making the team or not, life would go on.

Even stranger still was watching L.B. He was off by himself too, but instead of standing there alone he was pacing back and forth ... back and forth. He looked like a caged animal. And I couldn't be positive from where I stood, but I thought he was talking to himself.

L.B. was always so calm, but not now. I couldn't

figure out what he had to be nervous about. Not only was he a good player, but the coach was his father. It wasn't like he was going to be cut.

My mind spun around, trying to think who the cuts might be. I looked around trying to locate the two or three people who seemed to be most on the edge. I didn't see any of them. Why weren't they here already? If they were late, he'd cut them for sure even if he hadn't already made that decision ... or had the decision already been made? Had Coach Barkley made the cuts? At least those three kids were missing. There had been sixteen kids at the game. Sixteen kids who hadn't been cut. How many of us were now outside the gym waiting to go in? I tried to do a quick count. There were seven standing by the doors ... and two over by the fountain, and one just coming in ... and then L.B. and me. That made twelve and he said there were going to be twelve spots on the team. So that meant that everybody who was here had made it! Kia, and Jamie, and D.J., and Mark and Jordan and Brian and me! I'd made it. I was on the team. That was great ... wasn't it? For some reason I didn't feel that excited ... or relieved. Shouldn't I feel both of those emotions? Or at least one of them?

I wondered if anybody else had figured out that we were all on the team? If Kia had she would have said something to me. Judging from the expressions of the others, nobody else had worked it out. If they had they would have looked at least a little bit more excited about things.

The door opened and Coach Barkley appeared. He motioned for everybody to come in. There was a crush as everybody rushed the door. I wasn't going to be telling them anything now.

I turned around. L.B. was still standing off to the side. Maybe he hadn't seen his father call us in. I trotted over to him.

"Aren't you coming in?" I asked.

"In? Oh, is it time?" he asked.

"Everybody else is already inside so we better get going or we'll be late."

"We wouldn't want to keep my father waiting," he said.

"That's for sure. Come on," I said as I started for the door. Even if I was right and was on the team, I didn't want to get him mad at me.

Just as I got to the gym door I glanced over my shoulder. L.B. still wasn't coming. He was just staring off into the distance like he was looking at something.

"L.B.!" I called out. He looked at me but didn't move.

There was a strange look in his eyes. He looked scared. But what did he have to be scared of? Maybe he didn't know he was on the team. Maybe his father hadn't told him?

I jogged back to his side. "There's nothing to worry about," I said.

"What?" he asked.

"There's nothing to worry about. I'm completely positive that everybody who's here is on the team already."

"Yeah," he said absently. "That's what my father told me last night."

"So you already know that you're on the team, right?"

He nodded his head. "Everybody here will be offered a spot on the team."

"That's great," I said.

"Is it?" L.B. asked.

"Yeah ... sure ... of course ... I guess."

"Let's get inside," I said, grabbing L.B. by the arm to start him moving with me.

We entered the gym and everybody else was already sitting in the middle of the floor by the coach's feet. He looked over at us and scowled.

"Nice of you gentlemen to join us," he said. "You're both lucky this isn't our first try-out or it could have been your last."

"Sorry," I mumbled as I grabbed a piece of the floor beside Kia. L.B. sat down beside me.

"I'd like to start by stating the obvious," Coach Barkley said. "You'll notice that there are only twelve of you sitting in here today."

A number of heads spun around trying to quickly

126

do a head count to confirm what he'd said.

"And as some of you may recall there are twelve spots on this team. So those of you who aren't math-challenged will quickly come to a realization about why we're all here today."

"We're … we're on the team?" Jordan asked.

Coach Barkley smiled. "Close. You are all being *offered* a spot on the team."

"What does that mean?" Kia asked.

"It means that I'm going to outline what is expected of you if you decide to accept a spot on this team, because I want to make it perfectly clear that I'm going to demand a lot out of all of you. Who'd like to hear those expectations?"

Everybody either nodded their head or mumbled agreement.

"My first expectation is that players will be at all games and all practices unless they have a very valid reason for being absent. There will be one or two games every week, as well as practices on one or two nights. Each week will have a minimum of three nights of ball, with an expectation of more practices on the weeks before a tournament."

That was an incredible amount of basketball.

"In addition we'll be going to seven or eight weekend tournaments and some of those tournaments will involve driving to other cities and staying overnight."

What was my mother going to think about all of that I wondered.

"And further it is an expectation that those nights when you are not with me in the gym for either a practice or a game you will be working out on your own. Each of you will have a personal practice inventory."

"A what?" Jamie asked.

"A list indicating your weaknesses — areas of your game that you have to improve. The key to success isn't just practicing what you do well, but improving what you do badly."

I guess that made sense. It did sound like an awful lot of basketball.

"And if you think the try-outs were hard, you haven't seen anything yet. My practices will be brutal. And that game you played on Thursday ... that will be nothing compared to the intensity I'll *demand* from you once the season begins. You're going to be living, breathing, eating, sleeping, and talking about basketball for the next five months," he continued.

That wasn't really anything different than I usually felt, but somehow it didn't seem the same when somebody told me I *had* to feel that way. What if I didn't feel like playing basketball, or just wanted to hang around or watch TV?

"Now my question to each and every one of you is this, can you make that commitment to this team? If you can, then you're a member of the Magic. If you can't, you're free to walk."

Everybody started to mumble to each other when suddenly L.B. stood up. All at once all the noise stopped.

"What are you doing?" Coach Barkley asked him.

"Getting up and leaving," he said quietly.

A gasp went up — not only from the other kids, but from the coach.

"What do you mean you're leaving?"

"I don't want to be part of the team."

The coach's mouth opened, but no sound came out. He looked completely mystified.

L.B. started to walk away and that seemed to cause the coach's brain to unfreeze.

"You can't just walk away!" he called out.

L.B. looked back, gave a slight shrug of his shoulders and continued to walk. Apparently he could walk away. We all watched in shocked silence as he reached the door, pushed it open, and vanished.

I stood up.

"Don't go after him," Coach Barkley ordered. "He'll come back."

"No, you don't understand," I said, shaking my head. "I'm not going after him. I don't want to be on the team either."

I didn't even believe what I'd just said. It was like somebody else had spoken. I started walking

even though my legs were shaking so badly that I thought I might topple over. Was I crazy doing this or what?

I heard a sound and turned back toward the group. Kia had gotten up and was following me. Then Jamie and D.J. stood up and started after her ... then Mark, and Jordan, and then everybody got up.

I stopped at the door of the gym and waited while Kia caught up to me. The coach was standing in the center of the gym by himself. He looked so all alone.

Chapter Fourteen

I glanced at the clock on the wall. He'd be here in less then five minutes. I felt scared.

"We won't let him pressure you," my mother said.

"Pressure me?"

"Into being on the team. You made your decision and we're proud of you for taking a stand," my father said.

He'd been saying that a lot. At first I didn't understand or believe him. Why would he be proud of me for quitting? Especially if he thought that maybe I needed to be tougher? Since when was quitting being tough?

"We're just being polite, allowing him to come over and talk," my father continued.

"And he sounded so sad when he called," my mother added. "I almost felt sorry for him."

Great, that was just what I wanted to hear.

"Has he been to see anybody else yet?" my father asked.

"I don't know for sure. I do know he's going to see Kia and her parents right after us, and then D.J. and Jamie's families later on tonight."

"It sounds like he's really making the rounds," my mother said. "I'm still not sure why he's doing this."

"Maybe he wants to convince everybody to come back and give it another try," my father said. He sounded hopeful. Maybe he kept saying he was proud of me, but I knew he was also pretty disappointed that I wouldn't be playing basketball this year — except for maybe house league ball.

"Maybe he just wants to say he's sorry," I said.

"Len Barkley sorry?" my father questioned. "As a player he never backed down or said he was sorry or —"

"That was more than twenty years ago," my mother said, cutting him off. "Maybe he's grown up a little bit ... although judging from what I've seen and heard, he hasn't grown up very much."

"He can be a good guy," I said.

My parents both gave me a questioning look.

"That's what L.B. told us. He said that away from the gym his father is different ... way different. He said he was funny and fun."

"I've never seen that side," my mother said.

"I have," I said. "Just once, but I've seen it."

Just then the doorbell rang.

"I'll get it," my mother said, getting up and leaving my father and me at the table.

Suddenly that gnawing feeling in my stomach turned into a big block of cement. What would he say? Was he mad at me because I had been the first to follow L.B.? Was he coming here to yell at me and tell me that I was a big disappointment and a quitter? Then I looked over at my father.

He smiled and reached out to put a hand on my shoulder.

"There's nothing to worry about," he said. "Nobody, and I mean *nobody*, is going to bother my son as long as I'm here. Understand?"

I nodded my head. I knew he meant what he said. As long as he was sitting beside me I was safe from anything.

Coach Barkley walked into the kitchen, followed immediately by my mother. My father rose to his feet and offered his hand. The two men shook.

"I was saying to your wife what a lovely place you have here," Coach Barkley said.

"Thank you. My wife did all the decorating herself," my father answered.

"My wife and I are just itching to get started on our new house," he said. "We moved in just over from here."

"Nick had mentioned that," my mother said.

"We've been so busy that we haven't had much time, but I'm hoping we can get started decorating soon. I was looking at some wallpaper that had a matching fabric so I could reupholster the dining room chairs and then I thought I could add a chair rail."

"That sounds like it could be very attractive," my mother said. "I didn't know you had an interest in decorating."

"Neither did I," my father added in amazement.

"It's not the sort of thing that I mentioned too much in the old days," he admitted. "But I didn't come here to talk about decorating. I came here to apologize."

I looked at my father and he nodded. I'd been right about why he'd come to see us.

"There are things I said and did that I'm truly sorry for."

"We understand," my mother said. "And we appreciate you coming here to say that. This wouldn't have been easy."

"I've always tried to take the right route instead of the easy one, even if doing the right thing isn't pleasant." He paused. "I've always thought of myself as a pretty strong individual, but I don't think I would have had the guts to do what your son and my son did."

What did he mean?

"I don't think I would have ever had the strength to stand up and walk out the way the two of them did."

"Everybody walked out," I said, and then instantly regretted it. It sounded like I was rubbing it in.

"If you weren't brave enough to leave after my son did then nobody would have walked."

I still wasn't completely sure whether he was blaming me or giving me credit.

"I wouldn't have gone if it weren't for L.B. He was the brave one."

"You both were brave and I'm grateful for that. If you two hadn't walked out, then I might never have learned how wrong I have been. I never should have treated you boys that way. I was wrong."

"You weren't wrong about everything," I said.

He smiled. "I thank you for saying that, but I know I was wrong about all the important things. It's funny I've always considered myself a decent sort of man. I'm really not a bad guy."

"We know that," my father said.

"Although I had my doubts," my mother added. "But Nick told us about the things your son said about you."

"Things? I didn't know L.B. said anything about me."

Everybody looked at me. "He told me what a

good guy you are and how you like to joke around and have fun ... when you're not near a gym."

He smiled. "It was strange. I was gone from basketball for more than twenty years. I did a lot of growing up in that time."

"We all have," my father added.

"But you know, I got back in that gym and I can't quite explain it, but it was like all those years in between never happened. And it was exciting and scary all rolled into one big old ball. I got thinking about what it was like to play basketball and got more and more excited and before I knew it ... well you saw what happened." He paused. "And that's why I'm going to everybody's house tonight. I owe each and every child and their parents an apology. I thought because I was a pretty good player in my time that I could be a good coach."

"You were a good coach," I said. "I learned things."

He chuckled. "Things like how loud I could yell?"

"Things like how to position myself for rebounds better and where to go when I didn't have the ball, and keeping my legs straighter when I make jump shots."

"I guess I still know a few things about the game," he said.

"A lot of things."

"Thanks for saying that. That's made my night a little bit easier."

He rose from his seat and offered me his hand. He shook my hand and then my mother's and finally my father's.

"I better get going," he said.

"I just put on a fresh pot of coffee," my mother offered. "And I did some baking. Would you like to stay for a cup and a cookie?"

"Thank you very much for the offer. I really appreciate it, but I still have a number of people I have to see tonight."

"Another time perhaps," my mother offered. "Maybe you can come in some time when you're dropping your son off to play with Nick."

He gave a little smile. "I really appreciate the offer. I hope I can still be a good neighbor even if I couldn't be a good coach. Take care."

Once again he and my father shook hands and then he turned to leave the kitchen.

"Coach ... I mean Mr. Barkley."

He stopped and turned back around.

"You could still be both," I said.

"Both?"

"A neighbor and a coach. Didn't you tell us that you're only a loser when you give up trying?"

"My old coach ... your old coach, used to tell us that."

"I'd be willing to try again, if you would."

"You want *me* to be your coach?" he asked in amazement.

"Everybody does things wrong. We only call it a mistake if you don't learn from it," I said. "He told us that too," I said, turning to my parents.

"And you'd be willing to try again?" Mr. Barkley asked.

"If we could talk about how things would be different."

"Believe me, things would be different!"

"Would that be okay? Could I play?" I asked my parents.

My mother and father looked at each other. What were they going to say?

"I think that might be okay," my mother said.

"I'd like that, but it might be too late. A team with just one player isn't going to work."

"How about your son?" my father asked.

"He might be willing as long as I remember to treat him like my son instead of just a player."

"There may be more than just me and him," I said.

"Have you talked to anybody else about this?" my father asked me.

"I didn't even talk to *me* about any of this," I said. "At least not yet."

I'd be on the phone to Kia and then Jamie and D.J. the second Mr. Barkley was out the door.

My father walked Mr. Barkley to the door. As they disappeared down the hall I heard my father mention something about the time the two of them played against each other in high school.

"He seems like a very nice man," my mother said. "I'm surprised. He wasn't anything like I'd expected him to be."

"Do you think it could work?" I asked her. "Do you think there's a chance we could still have a team?"

"I don't know. A few minutes ago I didn't even think any of this was possible," she said with a shrug of her shoulders.

"And now?" I asked.

"It might still be a long shot, but you've always been pretty good at long shots."